Helen Dickens

The Mill Wheel

Vol. II

Helen Dickens

The Mill Wheel
Vol. II

ISBN/EAN: 9783337067137

Printed in Europe, USA, Canada, Australia, Japan

Cover: Foto ©Andreas Hilbeck / pixelio.de

More available books at **www.hansebooks.com**

THE VISCOUNT FIGANIÈRE'S NEW NOVEL.

In 3 Vols., 31s. 6d.

PALMITOS.

BY THE VISCOUNT FIGANIÈRE,

ENVOY EXTRAORDINARY AND MINISTER PLENIPOTENTIARY
AT THE IMPERIAL COURT OF RUSSIA.

" Palmitos is interesting, introducing us to what we suspect English people know very little about, country life in the Empire of Brazil. The book is decidedly entertaining."—*Athenæum*.

" We doubt if in 1874 a better, more interesting, or graphic novel will be published."—*Daily Guardian*.

" Life on a slave plantation is described with a vividness which is at times quite frightful. For an appreciative and sympathetic history of slavery the book deserves careful study. A charming heroine whose protests against cruelty and constant adventures add much to the thrilling interest with which it cannot fail to be read."—*John Bull*.

THE MILL WHEEL.

A NOVEL.

IN THREE VOLUMES.

BY

HELEN DICKENS,

Author of " Wild Wood," &c.

VOL. II.

LONDON:
T. CAUTLEY NEWBY, PUBLISHER,
30, WELBECK STREET, CAVENDISH SQUARE.
1874.

THE MILL WHEEL.

CHAPTER I.

WHEN Lady Rudkin and Rodney were finished, there was a general exhibition, and the verdict with one accord was " Splendid ; could not be better." They were hung in the gallery, my Lady occupying the place of the lost Clorinda. Sir Bevis was delighted, and, taking Rufus Sebastain into his study, wrote a cheque for the amount agreed upon. And it was not too much, for Rufus was still modest.

" And now I am at liberty, Sir Bevis ?"

" By no means, Mr. Sebastain ; Mrs. Howard

and myself are the next to be operated on, and I dare say there will be more patients by the time we are cured. Therefore, we may still hope to keep you amongst us, my boy," and the kind old gentleman held out his hand.

Renie and Lucy were very pleased to have the pleasant, intelligent man longer with them, and even little master baby pranced about when the news was made known.

A day or two following Rufus went to the Bank to get the cheque cashed, and did not appear till dinner time. The Count and Countess Helring were spending that evening at Zeigleheath, also Norman and Addy. There was a walk to be taken in the dusk, of course, and Norman, with a wicked twinkle in his eye, managed that the single people should go together. Lucy and the Count were having a fine time, and could be heard joking and laughing at a great pace. Rufus and Renie were quieter; Rufus was telling Renie his errand that day.

" And you know, Miss Rudkin, the half of the money is yours, because you painted the child. See," and he came to a standstill in the path, and drew a crisp roll of paper out of his pocket, " I have divided it ; your uncle gave me a hundred, and here is fifty ?"

The girl drew back from the outstretched hand, and eyed him in astonishment.

" Are you offended, Miss Rudkin ?" asked he in a low tone of pain.

" No," and the eyes glistened slightly ; " no, Mr. Sebastain ; but you have hurt me. I thought we were friends !"

" And are we not ?"

" Well, then, keep that money ; I do not want it, and you may. Moreover I would not take it if I were *starving*, there now."

The hand dropped to his side, and he replied rather mournfully—

" I know I cannot force you, Miss Rudkin ; but the money is rightfully yours, and I, too, am proud ; I do not ask charity."

"Stay, Mr. Sebastain, don't go off with a wrong notion. I spoke rudely, most probably, but I never was noted for either elegance or politeness, so you must not mind me. I beg your pardon."

"No, no, Miss Rudkin, no apology from you; it is I who ought to make one. But come, tell me, this money is yours; what am I to do with it?"

"Will you follow my directions?"

"Yes."

"Then I desire you to keep it and bank it; and promise me to add to it every quarter?"

"I do promise. I see what you want; you want me to work steadily, and not spend every shilling?"

"Exactly. I hope to see you a great man, Mr. Sebastain, and not always a beggar with nothing to turn to. Don't regard that money as a gift—it is not—it is a decoy. I am doing with you as they do with fowls, putting an egg in your nest to induce you to lay some more to it."

He grasped one of the brown hands, rolled up as usual, and wrung it.

"God bless you, Miss Rudkin; as the Spanish woman was my angel when a poor weary lad, so you are my angel and friend now, when I am a tempted, struggling man."

They looked all they might have said had not the Count, with gay Lucy on his arm, appeared at the turn of the poplars.

"Found at last," said the Count, displaying a row of white teeth, and extending a well-shaped hand, garnished with a magnificent ring, in the direction of the artist and Renie.

"They are all seeking you, Miss Rudkin !"

"Indeed! Then if you and Miss Northwood are assisting them, I presume you got lost yourselves in the attempt to find us ?"

"Now you are too bad, Miss Rudkin, only the paths are so secluded and intricate that once or twice Miss Northwood became confused; is not that so ?"

The handsome face wore the most wicked

expression of mischief, and the mouth smiled from side to side. If Lucy had not been as he said, "confused," before, she most assuredly was then, and actually could not look up, because she felt he was studying her face, highly amused.

The Count was a perfect gentleman, and knew when to stop; so he now returned to Renie, and said—

"My mother wants to know more of you, Miss Rudkin; she has not said six words to you."

He was too polite to say, "You have not said six words to her," which was the fact of the case.

The delicate lady with the silvered locks had been ready enough to chatter, only Renie had other fish to fry. She lifted up her honest face, and at once said—

"I am sadly remiss, Count, but I generally leave others to entertain guests when I can. I hope the Countess has not been neglected."

"Oh dear no ; only she has taken a great fancy to you."

Renie did not respond to this amiable sentiment, but Rufus did, under his breath, and coolly turning on his heel, murmured " How very gratifying."

Before the Count and Countess left, it was decided that the girls and Mr. Sebastain should walk over some afternoon soon, and take a good look at the curiosities of Chiverton.

The Countess gave them a cordial invitation, and assured them they would be conferring a favour upon her, for, cheerful and happy though she naturally was, yet she at times felt excessively dull when Carl was out.

One afternoon Renie thought it was high time she visited Mrs. Troost in her den, and accordingly, being requested by Lucy to get her some cake, departed. She found the worthy dame busy beating up eggs in a bowl, with her spectacles on.

" Why, it's Miss Renie I do declare. I quite thought you had forgotten your poor old Troost. Since this artist has been here you have been as scarce as mushrooms in November. And how's Miss Lucy ?"

" Quite well, Mrs. Troost," replied Renie, settling herself, " and she told me to be sure and not forget her cake."

" Ha, ha, ha !" laughed Mrs. Troost, " she knows it's late. These eggs is for it. Bless the child, how she does like them cakes. I had master baby here this morning, begging for crumpets. I don't know what my lady would say, if she knew it."

" By the way, Mrs. Troost, Christie tells us that there are some gipsies here. Is it true ?"

" Yes, Miss Renie, I believe so," replied Mrs. Troost, sighing. " It is many, many years since they gave us a turn. This is a grand tribe, I believe; you and Miss Lucy should get your fortunes told, Miss Renie."

" Well, we'll see about it.   But where are
they ?"

" Not far off ; in their old seat, the wood
at the back of the old water mill.   They have
their vans on the bank of the river, so Harry
says, and I suppose they cook and roam in
the woods.   The horses and mules are feed-
ing on the meadows."

" What will uncle say to that, I wonder ;
gipsies are not considered desirable neigh-
bours."

" Sir Bevis ?   He'll say nothing, Miss
Renie, not if they pitch their tents in the
park.   And these gipsies are not thieves ;
they and their fathers before them have always
had a plot of ground at Zeigleheath, and they
came regularly ever since I can remember
till many years ago, and all at once they
stopped, and everyone asked where the
gipsies were.   But they never came again,
and I never thought they would.   It gave me
a turn when all the servants began to cry out

' the gipsies are here.' It put me in mind, like that bell, of old days. It is more than twenty years since there has been a gipsy fire kindled at the back of the water mill, Miss Renie."

" Indeed ! You are as good as a directory, Mrs. Troost; you know pretty nearly everything."

" Yes, all that comes and goes in the Rudkin family. But you must remember I have lived here all my life, never served any other family, and I am sixty turned. Thank God for my good health. I am still able to keep order here, and I hope to do so for many years to come. But you young ladies should have your fortunes told, it is a bit of a joke. I saw the Count in the grounds the other evening; he is nice looking, Miss Renie; won't he do for you ?"

" Oh ! that's not the question ; it's will I do for him ? Do I look fit to be a Countess ? What should I do with these ?" and she spread out her two little brown hands.

" Never mind, Miss Renie," replied the old woman, eyeing them sorrowfully enough ; " notwithstanding, you are very nice and pleasant when you like, and we cannot all be beautiful."

" Just so ; but it is hard to make people understand that when there is no gold to fling in their eyes. I labour under two disadvantages, my good Mrs. Troost—poverty and plainness, and I am perfectly aware of them. I am only here by the kindness of uncle. I have no right to be here. I cannot expect anything now."

" That's true enough, Miss Renie; and when that baby was born I could have twisted it's neck, poor little innocent. I call it robbery, because you and Miss Addy was brought up with the idea that you would get whatever was over. However, I am glad for one thing, it will keep this grand old place in the Rudkin family, and Master Rodney promises to make a fine lad."

" Lucy," announced Renie, on her return,

" Christie is perfectly correct in her statement,
the gipsies are here ; a goodly tribe, all en-
camped by the old mill ; and your cake was in
course of preparation, and will be up to-
night."

" Hurrah for the gipsies ! they are a decided
change in the programme ; we will go and
have a peep at them, eh, Renie ?"

" Yes, if you choose ; Mrs. Troost wishes
us to have our fortunes told. I have never
visited a gipsy camp."

" No more have I. We shall have some
toothless old hag showing our fate on the
palm of our hands. I only hope she won't
spit on mine, or tell me I shall have great
sorrow and tribulation, and six children."

CHAPTER II.

AT dinner the gipsies were mentioned, and Sir Bevis seemed glad, and said he had seen them the day they arrived. The head of the tribe —the King—was a wonderfully powerful, handsome man.

Their advent was the cause of quite a commotion in the village, and nearly every maiden had had her fate mapped out, though they had been there only a day or two. They were not poor, they seemed to have plenty, and report said the king's tent and van had velvet pile carpets on the floors.

By the time dinner was over, Lucy's curiosity had arrived at such a pitch that nothing would do but they must set off there and then, but Renie stoutly refused till she had had some tea, which raised a hearty laugh.

Rufus Sebastain was to escort them, and ascertain his fate.

It was next door to dark as the three threaded their way over the bridge into the meadow, and along the river's bank to the water mill. Before they got near the camp dogs commenced to bark; not common curs, but great powerful beasts with hanging lips. Rufus Sebastain stopped by the vans to examine them, and immediately said—

" These are not English dogs, Miss Rudkin; they are the Spanish blood hound, and two pure ones."

The great creatures were tugging at their chains, and almost pulling the heavy vans in their frantic efforts to get at the three.

They were chained very short, and now and then, after a great but, fortunately, ineffectual pull, would stand on their hind legs, their eyes red with passion, and the saliva and froth dropping from the gaping jaws.

The vans seemed deserted, but in the wood could be seen the glare of a fire, and now and then a figure flitted through the trees.

"They are in the wood, Renie," said Lucy, "let us go, these brutes will be mad if we stay a second longer. I would as soon approach a lion as one of these."

Lucy was not the only one pleased to move, and a few strides brought them to the wood.

The Mill house was empty, and had been for long, and the wood was nearly smothered with creepers and trees. The steps that led to the door were green and slimy, and every plank gaping. The place was picturesque, especially now, with the light of the fires dancing upon it. The only sound was the dash of water, as the wheel turned round and round.

Again the two came to a standstill, and they were not the only standers. On the tumble-down old stage far out in the stream, close by the busy wheel, stood a girl, leaning over the rail and gazing into the water. Her face was turned, and she appeared absorbed in thought. Perhaps the rush of the river prevented her hearing.

Once more matter-of-fact Lucy called the two artists to order, for they were drinking in the beauties of the scene.

"Well, are we to stand here all night? Don't say that girl has bewitched you, Mr. Sebastain, for there's nothing to be seen but the back of her head, a pair of legs, and a scarlet petticoat. Sir Bevis will think they have run off with us, or thrown us to those dragons of dogs, if we stay much longer."

"Capital advice, Miss Northwood, you would make an excellent commanding officer, the way you give the order to march is unrivalled. There would not be many flights of imagination with you present."

They again started forth, and this time really reached the camp without any stoppages. They did not at once make their presence known, but took a survey of the gipsies. There were two or three fires, all blazing cheerily, and in the flames of one, suspended on three sticks, was the pot bubbling and spitting forth a most savoury odour. Some birds were roasting on a rod and an old woman, with wild eyes and straggling gray locks, bent nearly double with age, plunged her skinny hand from time to time into the ashes and felt the potatoes, to try if they were done. The others were squatted round the fires, some smoking, while others gambled for bits of silver.

A handsomer, wilder set never was looked at ; the men were tall supple fellows in tight leather gaiters, and with some sort of a girdle round their waists. They were all dark as night, with bronzed clear faces and glistening teeth. They were evidently conversing, for suddenly there would be a burst of laughter, and the hag would stop stirring the kettle and glance round to see what was the matter. But there was not much noise; the mirth commenced after supper. The women were of the genuine Zingara type, with long black hair hanging over their shoulders. Some carried children in their arms, and some older ones were grouped under a tree quarrelling. Conspicuous from the rest, with the fire light full on him, was a man seated on a keg, in moody silence. He was of great stature with long hair and a beard that hung almost to his feet, of black well mixed with white, and a dark green beaver hat, with high crown and broad flaps, was cocked on one side of his head. His dress corresponded pretty nearly with that of the others, with the exception that, slung across his wide chest by a chain, was a silver horn or bugle. He was the king, the chief of the tribe. The three now made a move out of the shade, but before they had taken a step, the gipsies were all on their feet, and a thundering voice called "Hold!"

"Pilgrim Fathers!" ejaculated Lucy; "this seems serious."

"Don't be frightened," said Rufus, "we shall have to explain our errand to the Chief, I suppose."

The great fellow came stalking along, cracking every stick he set his foot on, and halted before the three, whom he almost burnt with his piercing eyes. There was something so free and proudly dignified in his mien, and then he was such an imposing man, standing over six feet, strong and straight. He looked at them in the dim light given by the fires (for they were some distance off), searchingly, and then said shortly—

"Your business?"

The girls afterwards confessed to being

terrified, and even Rufus Sebastain took a
second before he replied. They looked such
a fearless, lawless set to venture amongst.
But there was no going back.

The giant stood like a pillar of granite in
front of them, and all his men ready at a
word to do his bidding.

"Our business is harmless enough; we
want our fortunes told."

"Oh!" and he smiled a little, and bent to
get a better look at Rufus. "Come this
way."

The men and women eyed them from head
to foot, and Lucy persisted in keeping very
close to Renie. At a sign from the Chief
they all fell back, and left them alone by the
cracking fire.

"Do you want your fortune told?" asked
the King, turning to Renie.

"Yes," replied she, gazing into the handsome face, which did not look so hard now;
"we all do."

He smiled again, and called Ursula.

The old crone cooking came hobbling towards them, a very sight to behold. She quickly comprehended what she was wanted for, and mumbling something about " pretty lady," drew Lucy on one side and took her hand, which, to that young lady's intense relief, she did not spit into, but did on to the shilling, and crossed her hand with it. Lucy's fortune was highly satisfactory, so it would seem, for she joined the group by the fire with a pleased face.

" Now, Miss Rudkin," said Rufus, " it is your turn."

The gipsy started at the name, and asked—

" You are Miss Rudkin, the daughter of the owner of the land we are on ?"

" No, not daughter, niece—my father was Colonel Rudkin," and Renie passed on to old Ursula.

The Chief eyed her curiously, and, muttering something to himself, half turned from the others and kept silent.

The old fortune-teller was not so speedy over arriving at Renie's fortune, and when she returned to the rest she was not so well pleased as Lucy. Rufus Sebastain was served last, and then the old crone hobbled to them, and in a squeaky voice charged them not to repeat what she had told them for twelve months; they could relate what she had predicted for them any time after that period that they chose, but not a day before.

"Mind," said she, pointing a skinny forefinger at Rufus Sebastain, "mind you, fair one, Brag's a good dog, but Holdfast's a better."

They now turned to leave the camp, and the Chief took off his hat, and in the most courtly manner returned their bows.

"What a princely fellow," exclaimed Lucy, when out of ear shot. "I never saw such a collection of handsome men in all my life. They have put the extinguisher on the Life Guards, in my estimation."

"I really don't wonder at your saying it,

Miss Northwood. I have never met their equal. They are certainly no ordinary band of gipsies. I wonder where they come from. Spain or Portugal I should say. The Chief seemed to know your family, Miss Rudkin."

"Yes. The housekeeper told me that they have been in the habit of coming for years and years. And all at once, more than twenty years since, they disappeared, and nothing has been seen of them up to the present time. My grandfather never interfered with them, and they knew they would be welcome to Zeigleheath. It was a wonderful scene when first we looked through the trees. Can't you paint it, Mr. Sebastain?"

He smiled.

"Yes, I daresay I could; but it is very rarely these gipsy scenes get justice done to them. But we might try together if you like."

CHAPTER III.

FOR about five minutes after they had departed, the Chief stood looking into the red
fire without moving a limb. He was talking
to himself in a foreign tongue, and several
times the name of Rudkin slipped from
between the teeth.

Presently he wheeled round, for he felt
something touch him. He was not mistaken.

There, at his elbow, stood a female huddled
up with only a white agonised face and bands
of snow white hair peeping from under the

thick hood. The lips remained parted in speechless agony, and one thin, delicate hand clutched his girdle nervously.

"Hagar! Hagar! what is it?" asked the man, catching her hand. "What is it?"

"Hush! hush!" said she, glancing round fearfully, "Aaron!" and the thin hand twisted itself out of his, "Aaron! do the dead come back?"

The Chief started from her in horror.

"No, no," said he, soothingly, drawing her nearer, "they don't come back, or else—Hagar, have you been dreaming?"

"No, Aaron, no; I have been wide awake," and she put her hands to her head; "I was sitting in the doorway of the tent yonder, and, looking up suddenly, I saw standing by this fire a figure, and that figure had the face of—. Oh, Aaron, am I never to be at peace? Is my sin to chase me for ever? My soul has been in hell for years and years; it is in hell now. Oh, if I could only die to-night and forget it all."

Her voice had risen to a wail of pain, and she shook like a leaf.

"Hush! don't let them hear you," and he put his arms round the trembling creature.

"Hagar! wife! look up. What is it you fear? No one shall take you while I live; you are safe here."

"Yes, I know I am," replied she, clinging to him; "it is my conscience, Aaron; if I could only forget."

A light step at that instant became audible, and the King said, quickly—

"Here's our child."

A young girl came bounding through the trees, and stopped at their side.

"Father?"

"Well, my daughter," replied he, bending down to kiss the beautiful face.

It was the girl Renie and the others had seen leaning over the mill-rail, on their way to the camp. Althea was as beautiful as a dream, about eighteen; and the only child of Aaron and Hagar, the gipsy King and Queen. Her father adored the sweet young thing, and blessed the very ground her little foot trod on.

She was like him, dark; with a soft, clear skin, and the most splendid pair of large, dreamy, languid eyes.

Her features were exquisitely delicate, like her form, and her hair, which streamed in a wavy mass over the marble shoulders, was of a blueish black tint, like the plumage of the raven, and as soft and glossy as silk. Her dress was peculiar, being composed of a black velvet bodice laced across the chest, a scarlet cloth petticoat, blue silk stockings and shoes; and on her head a kerchief of scarlet silk, richly embroidered with gold.

"Father," said Althea, "I saw some people go along the river bank; have they been to see Ursula?"

"Yes, Althea; they came to have their fortunes told."

"I hope she told them pretty ones. May Ursula tell me mine, father?"

"No, my daughter, she may not tell the Princess Althea her fortune."

The girl made no further remark, but lifted her sweet face to be kissed again, while the eyes said plainly, "Don't be angry." The gipsy kissed her with a softened, loving face, but he did not relent and give the desired permission. And Althea knew her father too well to press the subject further. They all knew that when the King commanded they must obey.

By this time supper was ready, and they all partook of it in groups. The Chief and his family had a fire to themselves; several casks had been rolled from behind the thickets and as their contents passed round with no niggard hand, the mirth grew boisterous, and songs echoed through the silent wood till

tired out they fell asleep, some with their
drinking cups in their hands. The huge fires
roared, and crackled, and glared upon the
dark, sleeping forms stretched round them
through the still autumn night.

But all did not sleep; their Queen lay in
her tent softly sobbing to herself, till the pale
light of day glimmered through the tree tops,
and the woodland birds sent up a sweet song
of praise to their Maker.

CHAPTER IV.

ONE morning Lady Rudkin suddenly awoke
to the necessity of Rodney having a French
nurse.   Sir Bevis looked aghast, but my lady
insisted, and carried her point, to the no small
amusement of Rufus Sebastain.

The old baronet said it was absurd, and so
it was; but notwithstanding my lady advertised or applied to some agent, and her efforts
were crowned by the arrival of a young
woman with a peculiar expression of face,
who spoke patois, and that was Lady Rudkin's
idea of good French.   Nurse Mary did not

make the least objection to the presence of
Sedorice Dumont, and they soon became
friends. Many were the laughs she had at
poor Sedorice's expense, and good quiet Mary
was rather shocked to hear her teaching
Rodney the 23rd Psalm one day, the second
verse of which she rendered as follows, " He
maketh me to lie down in green plasters."

This was too much for even sober Mary's
gravity, and she laughed heartily. But
Sedorice was of an excellent temper, and did
not take offence at anyone. She loved the
boy, and everyone in the house, excepting the
male-cum-female Shepperton. They quarrelled
dreadfully, and Sedorice, when excited beyond
control, would shriek at the top of her voice
at the sneaking monster.

Things wore the same aspect as formerly;
the pictures were progressing, and the gipsies
still held court at the water mill.

When asked how he liked such a quiet life,
Rufus Sebastain would make answer—

"Very much, because a settled home or a sure meal had not been his fate before."

His face had not that hunted look so often now as when first he came, and he did not express himself quite so bitterly. The rest and peace were calming his soul, poor fellow!

It is all very well to admire those who are noted and have a name, but all the adoration that the earth can produce is but poor recompense for the weary toil and struggling. Fame is dearly purchased, and the cost never forgotten. It requires no little amount of determination and hope to wade through the sea of trouble and despair which lies directly in the path of every poor friendless genius. And when you reach the opposite shore, and pause to take breath, you feel very differently to when you commenced the journey. The joy and freshness of life is gone, you have left it behind you, and I don't know that all the glory makes up for the feeling of weariness.

We are told that "Gold must be tried by

fire, as a heart by pain." It may answer for the gold, but it is a mistake with the heart. I cannot speak well of the refining process. Your heart comes out of the furnace in pretty much the same condition as an egg which a rat has sucked, there is nothing left but the shell.

The winter seemed close at hand, especially in the evenings, and the great house began to feel chilly.

My lady was a great one for creature comforts, so after dinner a fire was lighted at one end of the drawing-room, in case she might feel cold.

The tatting did not progress favourably, and many a time was Lucy to be seen on her knees patiently teaching the laughing lady.

One evening this was the case, and they were alone in the room, Renie and Rufus were out, and Sir Bevis writing letters.

"Now look, Lady Rudkin, under, over, make a loop, so!"

How long this interesting occupation might have lasted there is no telling, had Lucy's eyes not been addicted to roving, as in the days at Hill Cottage. The only difference being that there she saw little of consequence, if anything, and invariably got punished for her pains, whereas at Zeiglcheath she did see something, especially this evening. Her eyes made a rapid circuit of the large room, and rested on a window directly facing the fire-place, and there they became fixed!

Pressed close to the glass was the face of a man, a pale, haggard face, with black, prominent eyes. He was gazing at Lady Rudkin in a bewildered way, and seemed almost petrified.

So intent was he, that it was not until Lucy had given a loud scream, and pointed to him, that he understood, and moved away.

"My dear Miss Northwood," exclaimed Lady Rudkin, jumping up, "whatever is the matter?"

" Oh, Lady Rudkin, did you not see that man ?"

" Man ? no ! Where is he ?"

" Gone now, he was watching us through that window, and he terrified me when I looked up. He was looking at you !"

" At me ?" said my lady, starting. Then added, with her usual laugh, " it must have been one of the new servants, or perhaps Mr. Sebastain coming back from the village !"

" No," retorted Lucy, composedly, " it was a strange face, and a startling one, too ! It was a handsome face, with large, dark eyes, a thin, pale face !"

By the time Lucy stopped, every vestige of colour had deserted my lady's face, and the shuttle dropped from her nerveless fingers.

" Assuredly," continued Lucy, proceeding with her defence, it was not Mr. Sebastain, for he and Renie returned some ten minutes ago ; I heard them laughing as they passed through the hall. But, Lady Rudkin, I have frightened you, how thoughtless of me," and Lucy's hand was extended to the bell.

"No, no, Miss Northwood, by no means, I am perfectly well, only timid. Sir Bevis laughs at me, but I always was, from a child. I think I will go upstairs for a little," and, suiting the action to the word, she departed in great haste, so it seemed to Lucy.

Barely had the one door closed than the other opened to admit Renie and Rufus Sebastain. The artist might reasonably have been called her shadow, for you rarely saw one without the other. It was queer how he clung to the plain quiet girl; he appeared to think all safe if Miss Rudkin was at hand, and he asked her opinion and advice about his pursuits and projects as a brother would have done.

They came in talking in a wise, grave manner, and made straight for the fire, before which Lucy was standing.

" Why, Lucy, what is to do, my dear, you look frightened ?"

" Ah, I am recovering now, Renie, but I have had my heart turned inside out a few moments since."

" What with, Miss Northwood ?" enquired Rufus, stretching his hands to the blaze.

Lucy without more ado recounted the adventure of the face at the window, and then glanced at the other two. The artist was gazing into the fire, but a cynical smile played round the mouth.

" Lucy, did you see the face distinctly ?"

" Yes, and I believe I should be able to tell it again, but you must allow for the altera- tion caused by the nose being flattened against the window-pane. Whoever he was, he was staring at Lady Rudkin, and so absorbed was he, that I believe I escaped his notice. Which I can't say I regret ; I should not care to be the object of such flattering attentions. The idea struck me that he knew Lady Rudkin, and I cannot divest myself of it.   It was the expression of his face, it bespoke so plainly astonishment ; there was a sort of mute recognition impossible to describe."

"Nevertheless I comprehend your meaning, Miss Northwood," said the artist, with his eyes on Renie's face. "Did Lady Rudkin see him ?"

"No, but I described him to her, and shortly after she went upstairs."

It was a pity Miss Lucy, with her quick eye, could not have seen what my lady did when she got upstairs. She never tottered or trembled in the least, but made straight for her boudoir, the bell of which she pulled violently, and remained standing with it in her hand till it was answered by her maid Shepperton. She did not speak, the grim woman seemed to understand her business, for quickly securing the door, she advanced and said—

"Well ?"

" I think it is ' well,' " rejoined my lady, letting her hand drop at her side. " It has come at last, Shepperton. Ah ! " groaned Lady Rudkin, squeezing her hands together, " why did I relax guard one instant, one hour ? why did I not have the shutters closed ? I was a fool to forget that though I could not see out into the darkness they could see in."

The tall gaunt woman before her never moved a muscle till she said—

" That *was* a clever move of yours, my lady; I thought you were wiser than *that*. How long is it since you saw him ?"

" About ten minutes. But I did not see him, it was that shrewd Miss Northwood ; she sees everything. I wish I could put those girls' eyes out. And she can put two and two together. She suspects me of something, Shepperton ; she took care to say ' He was staring at you.' "

" I wonder what's to be done now, my lady, since you've managed *this* so cleverly ?"

" You must just go out and find him ; that girl's eyes may be at fault, and I cannot rest till I know the worst."

Shepperton laughed.

" That's not so easy got at. These people are so proud, they live on their pride, nothing else seems to move them. Don't you get treading on the old gentleman's corns, my lady, or he'll cut up rough; so you'd best leave the worst to take care of itself, and don't you stay up here too long, else you will have all their eyes and ears open."

Shepperton's advice was not to be despised, so my lady took herself back to the drawing-room, and the maid set out for a moonlight ramble. But her pains were not rewarded ; and after a vigilant scrutiny of all the place, and a peep into the " Cock and Trumpet " in the village, she resolved to return home.

Mrs. Shepperton was little known, if at all, in Moordart, for she adopted the bat's plan, and only took her airings at night. It was astonishing, though, how much she had learnt by these perambulations. She knew every twist and turn, every little alley and short cut, every public and private path. So, after making her patrol, she returned to her mistress and informed her, with becoming serenity, that it was a fancy of Miss Northwood's; in short, it was not the party they were interested in.

But to appease my lady was not to appease Miss Northwood; that young lady resolved in future to keep her eyes and ears peeled. It was not her business, and she knew it.

"But, my beloved Renie, mysteries always had a curious charm for me; I can keep as silent as the grave, but I like to watch the turn of events, and in this instance I intend to. And there is no telling but what it may be useful."

"There is no mystery that I can see. A man, some tramp, or, more probably, one of the gipsies, looks into the drawing-room; there it begins and there it ends."

Lucy smiled.

" Not so fast, Renie ; it does *not* end there by a great way—in fact, we have just got to wait for the end. But it was no tramp's face, nor yet a gypsy's. My eyes are good, better than people might imagine ; and, for another thing, why need Lady Rudkin have turned so deadly pale when I described the face ? Had I said red hair and blue eyes, she would not have been suddenly seized with timidity. No, my unsuspecting Renie ; all is not on the square, my lady's conscience is not as spotless as her neck."

Renie eyed Lucy in astonishment.

" You are appearing in a new character, Lucy ; they should enrol you at Scotland Yard. Is this your first case ?"

" Yes ; I have learnt my business since I came here, Renie, and I positively like it. But don't be uneasy, I know how far to go."

CHAPTER V.

THE post bag was not as interesting an event at Ziegleheath as in some houses. There were no love letters; a good number of general letters always arrived, but never anything startling, and Lady Rudkin had only had one epistle since Lucy came. Her anxiety to behold the contents of the bag remained unabated, however, and it was a pity such constancy should go unrewarded.

At the fag end of breakfast the letters were read at table, and this morning Sir Bevis had a goodly pile. The last one, however, seemed to be difficult to read, for he held it before his eyes for at least ten minutes, during which period he coughed and fidgetted on his chair in a very unusual manner. At last the stopper came out, and his surprise burst in fragments round the table.

" Well, this is one of the oddest things I ever knew; after all these years to turn up at last. Renie, my dear, you are richer than I thought. You have one more relation—but stay, that is not true, he is no earthly relation to either you or me. Well! one connection the more. He addresses himself to me, and proposes to pay me a visit soon, so that we may become acquainted. It is an astonishing thing, since he is of so Christianlike a spirit, that he never hunted me up before."

"Yes, it is queer, uncle, but perhaps he is in the neighbourhood. When does he come ?"

" Let me see," said the old gentleman, putting up his eye-glass. " 'I purpose seeing you on the 26th.' Why, bless me! that's to-day, Renie, and he writes from Harley End. Better ask him to stay a few days, I suppose; the shooting is not nearly over, so Whitton tells me. By-the-way, why don't you go out with Norman Howard, Mr. Sebastain?"

" I don't think I am as good a hand with a gun as with a brush, Sir Bevis, and my work must not be hindered too much."

" Oh, pray don't go and leave us, Mr. Sebastain," said my lady sweetly, from behind the urn, "and Christmas coming!"

" No, nonsense, Sebastain; do as Lady Rudkin tells you," replied Sir Bevis. " We can't spare you this side Christmas. When you have painted everybody with a respectable countenance, you can take to teaching these girls to daub a bit, eh, Lucy?"

" Nothing I should like better, thank you ever so much," said Lucy, frankly. " But I don't think Mr. Sebastain *could* teach me to make any creature without bandy legs, or any eyes without a glide. I can do a nose, but not eyes."

Sir Bevis laughed heartily.

"That is a candid confession, Lucy, and you shall certainly not paint my picture, for it would shock me inexpressibly to find myself squinting. Renie, are you like Lucy?"

There was a dead pause, and Rufus Sebastain's mouth twitched dangerously, but Renie looked calmly at him while answering—

"No, I don't think I am quite so bad; but I will show you some of my attempts the next time you visit our studio, and then you can judge for yourself."

"Yes," continued Rufus, with a mischievous twinkle in his fine eye; "if Miss Rudkin is not present, I shall have much pleasure in acting showman, Sir Bevis."

"Ah! quite a conspiracy, I perceive. Pray is my friend Lucy a party to it?"

"Yes; I must plead guilty, and ask to be recommended to mercy. But I have had my

mouth literally stitched up ; my tongue has
not been my own since I came here, so you
must not be hard upon me, Sir Bevis."

" That I readily promise, Lucy, on condition that you regain possession of that useful
member, and turn it to my account. But now
about this new importation ; I don't know what
he is like, most probably a character and peculiar, for he was always from a boy a wanderer.
He has been from one pole to the other, I
suppose. But we must put up with his
vagaries, and you young people must take
him about if he stays, for he is sure to be
very active and fond of exercise. We must
have some parties while he is here, my love,
if he is presentable."

" Do you think he is a wild man, Sir
Bevis ?"

" I hope not, Lucy ; but he is sure to be
odd ; all travelled men with no fixed pursuit
are, and he never earned sixpence in his life.
His father left him a small patrimony, and

his mother so adores this son that she, poor
creature, has lived a secluded life to enable
this man to indulge his fancies, and play my
gentleman."

" Is he good looking, uncle ?"

" Indeed I don't know, Renie, I never set
eyes on him ; he is not old, I know that, for
he was not born till long after your father.
He is about thirty-nine or forty, certainly not
more."

" And is he married ?"

" That I don't know, either ; he makes no
mention of a wife, so I am inclined to believe
him single. Men of his roving propensities
don't generally marry, they find it incon-
venient as well as expensive to drag wives
and children after them round the world.
And they are always, as a rule, pinched for
money. No; I am prepared for a wild,
clumsy, gruff fellow, with a head like Diver's
back, and his face covered with bristles, who
will smoke and spit eternally. I am not

afraid of either of you falling in love with him, my dears, and I request Mr. Sebastain not to provoke him, as he is pretty certain to be violent and powerful."

" Goodness, Sir Bevis, I feel terrified ; you might be preparing us for the visit of some wild beast," replied his wife, with her eyes wide opened.

The old gentleman laughed.

" Well, my dear, we shall see ; I am only anticipating a little."

Which was perfectly correct, only it was anticipation all the wrong way. Sir Bevis drew his inference from surroundings, and for this once, at least, they did not tally with the central object.

It was not an overdrawn picture of a wanderer, a man who frittered his life away half on sea half on land ; but, alas ! the artist had not seen his model. The best disposed people frequently make mistakes, not out of wilfulness, but ignorance. We are very much creatures of imagination, and too often see one half and imagine the other. No one knew when he would arrive, and no one thought of watching for him.

The studio was a scene of much laughter and industry, as usual; Sir Bevis was getting his eyes painted in, and Miss Lucy not being the presiding genius, they did not look round the corners. Suddenly Rufus Sebastain laid down his brush, and turned to Renie.

"By the way, what is this new gentleman's name; I did not hear it?"

Renie looked at Lucy and Lucy at Renie, and both burst into a laugh.

"I don't wonder at you, Mr. Sebastain, for uncle never told us, and I forgot to ask. How excessively stupid; the creature must have a name, unless he disposed of it at the north pole. This is a new feature in the case, and decidedly novel, if we have to entertain a gentleman who has unfortunately left his name behind him. I have a good mind to go and ask uncle."

"No, never mind, Miss Rudkin, we shall hear it soon enough. I suppose he'll arrive in time for dinner?"

But Rufus, like Sir Bevis, was wrong in his supposition.

"It is half-past twelve," cried Lucy, "let us go and take a stroll before luncheon. It is a shame to neglect this bright day. We shall not have many more."

Lucy carried her point, and soon the three were running downstairs. From the terrace there came the sound of voices, and little Rodney called out—

"Aunty Renie, tum here."

The child was playing about with his papa and mamma, outside of the morning room window, and it was a happy picture.

The old man, with his white head bent to the baby's sunny one, and the young mother idly leaning against the stonework in her pretty morning costume, with a bunch of moss roses in her hand.

D 2

It was the sort of picture to dream about, and wonder how long it would last. Ah! it was passing then, fading like the summer, and autumn, with its tints of decay, was clasping them, as well as the trees, in its arms. Summer would return, and the sun pour down a golden flood, but it would never shine on those it shone on then. We cannot keep the flowers that bloom in summer, and we may not keep God's flowers. It would not be well; our Heavenly Father never strikes in anger, and many a time, as we watch the course events have taken after what we have considered a cruel blow, we may say from our hearts—

> "Oh! not in cruelty, not in wrath,
>   The Reaper came that day;
> 'Twas an angel visited the green earth,
>   And took the flowers away."

Renie obeyed master baby's call, and he politely invited her to dance with him, a performance which consisted of a series of plunges and jumps, holding by his aunt's

print dress, to the detriment of its gathers.
But Renie made no serious objection, and the
dance was gone through, to the great amusement of the spectators.

The little fellow, with his glittering, rum-
pled head, and gleaming eyes, was still clutch-
ing her dress, when a figure appeared on the
grass before them. He had no doubt arrived
during the dance, and no one had any eyes to
waste upon him. Though it would not have
been exactly waste, as everyone looks at anything out of the common, and this was an
uncommon specimen of the *genus homo.*
He advanced towards the group, alternately
eying Sir Bevis and Renie in a cool, nonchalant
manner, and without the slightest particle of
confusion.

The old Baronet muttered—

" It must be him !" and forthwith stepped
forward and held out his hand to "him !"

" You are the writer of a letter I received

this morning—a far off connexion of my
family ?"

" Yes, Sir Bevis ; I am that person, Leopold
Gunstan ; and this, I suppose, is Lady
Rudkin ?"

His eyes rested on Renie, who, with the
child clinging to her skirts, stood close to her
uncle.

" No," said Sir Bevis, smiling, " this is my
niece, Miss Rudkin ; *that* is my wife."

There was a scarcely perceptible lifting of
the bushy eyebrows as he bowed to the lady
indicated.

My lady was in a strange attitude ; lolling
against the massive stone corner in a half in-
dolent, half pettish manner, like a child, with
her pretty brows knitted. The sun was
shining full on her, perhaps she could not
see distinctly, anyway it imparted a queer
shade to her face.

She smiled faintly, and bent her head, then
shrunk further into the corner and shaded her

eyes with her hand. The roses that a few moments ago were a marvel of exquisite beauty were now a shapeless mass, lying at her feet, and sending up out of their mangled condition a breath of rich perfume, as if to call forth shame on their murderer, whose delicate hands had crushed them to death.

No one seemed to pay any attention to my lady, or to Miss Northwood, who, after bowing to the stranger, had been regarding him with a stern face. This man was the centre of attraction, and well he might be.

Leopold Gunstan, the wanderer, was a likely man to wander from sight, but not from mind. He had arrived at a state of perfection, he was what they term in shops "hand made." He was just a piece of machinery which could not be improved upon. He had not one ounce of flesh too much on his bones, or one drop of blood too many in his body. He looked as if he had been in training all his life, and as if nothing on earth could make him colour, or a drop of perspiration start to his brow. Had a cannon gone off at his back he would have taken his time to turn round. Where were Sir Bevis's anticipations ? where the head like Diver's back, and the face covered with bristles ? The man leaning in such a perfect position for showing his figure against the pillar that bright September morning had no roughness about him, either in speech, person, or manner. He seemed to have had his heart and mind, as well as his body, smoothed out with a flat iron, and he would slip round the world as silently and easily as an eel, never staggered, never at a loss for an excuse. His appearance was good ; it was distinguished to a certain degree, beyond that you got mystified as to his rank in life. He could pass for a good many things if you gave him his cue. Just the sort of man to do an immense amount of mischief without implicating himself in the least.

It is a great pity such angelic demons can't

be swept off the face of the earth, or be
born with turned eyes and flat noses. Leopold Gunstan was as handsome as the devil
ever painted any of his children. He was
tall, with broad shoulders, and a regular line
down the middle of his back, on each side of
which the muscles stood out in great swells.
His feet were long and cased in faultless
boots tied with tassels on the instep. His
hands, like his feet, were beautifully shaped
and white. His hair was cut in military
fashion close to his head, parted down the
centre and brushed flat ; his face, which was
particularly pale, was clean shaved, with the
exception of a silken black moustache and
imperial. His mouth was well shaped, and
when he smiled showed a good strong set of
teeth ; his eyes prominent and dark, had a
lazy, indifferent expression in them which
made you wonder if he were tired.

He talked to Sir Bevis and Renie, and
made overtures of friendship to Rodney, who

resisted with all his might, and set up a
dismal howl, with his arms locked round
Renie.

" Perhaps Miss Rudkin will kindly persuade
him to be friends with me ?"

And the manner said, "*you* cannot resist
me."

" Indeed, no, Mr. Gunstan ; I decline to be
peacemaker," said blunt Renie.   " I don't
know anything of you myself yet, so I can't
recommend you to the child. He must just
follow his own inclinations, and if he won't
make friends with you, it's no great sin."

Rufus Sebastain smiled ; the wanderer had
evidently not expected such a matter-of-fact
answer ; a blush and an attempt to conciliate
the boy would have been more to his mind.

" But don't you think, Miss Rudkin," and
he smiled listlessly, " that a little compulsion,
a little subordination, would be good to
bend the child's will, to form him after a set
pattern ? He cannot have an opinion of his

own yet, he does not know what he likes or dislikes."

"You think not? Rodney, my pet, look at this gentleman, he wants to see your eyes," and she lifted him in her arms up close to the dark face. "He wishes to be friends with you; what do you say to him?"

The pretty lad looked at him with a pouting mouth, and then said, in decided baby fashion—

"Vot Sedorice say to Shepperton, *vous bait.*"

And immediately turned and clapped his flushed little cheek against Renie's round one. This was a decided shock, but Leopold Gunstan did not give it up. He next appealed to the mother.

"Lady Rudkin, pray aid me; your charming little boy won't be friends with me; don't you think he might?"

As readily and submissively as a dog obeys its master did Lady Rudkin obey the wish of this strange man. She came forward and said—

"Renie, please put him down; Rodney, make friends with this gentleman directly."

But no, the Rudkin determination was in that baby in spite of his yellow head, and a look of delight shot over his father's face.

He set out his two chubby feet, and stood with set lips like a little dummy before his mother.

Renie was flushing just a trifle; she would not have the child forced into liking the cool, freezing man, or saying he did either. Something of what was passing in her mind showed itself in her face, and caught her uncle's eye.

Things had run smoothly up to now, and he did not care to have a rupture between positive Renie and his young wife. So he adhered to that widely known proverb, "A stitch in time saves nine," and hastened to the rescue.

"Esther, my dear, this is not a matter to call forth power; the child is not quite struck by Mr. Gunstan's stern face, and declines to be embraced. That is the fact of the case, and now we will dismiss it. Rodney, my boy, go to nurse."

The child ran off, very glad to be released, but the cloud on his mother's face deepened, as a half-pitying, half-cynical smile curved under the black moustache.

Lucy was looking on the while, assisted by Rufus Sebastain.

Renie got very tired of the scene and the actors, so coolly stepped on to the grass and made for the river. She heard others follow her example, and the terrace was deserted when she turned round. Sir Bevis and Lady Rudkin, with Leopold Gunstan, had disappeared through the window, and Lucy and Rufus Sebastain were some little distance behind her, talking earnestly.

"Stay, Renie, called Lucy, let us get up to

you. Here you are, Miss Rudkin, as cool as a cucumber, after nearly causing a mutiny."

"A mutiny! what do you mean? I could not say the child was in the wrong, when I would have done the same myself. And I am not going to be bashful and silent, just because a rather handsome man chooses to look at me."

"No, indeed, Renie; you spoke like a book, and certainly roused Mr. Gunstan; a few seconds more and I should have joined you. I could pull that man of iron to pieces with pleasure, were it possible, sneaking wretch!"

"Lucy, you are angry, what did he say to offend *you?*"

She half laughed.

"Nothing, only my lips itched to denounce him. This *is* a queer world, and your kind old uncle has opened his door to a wolf in sheep's clothing this time, Renie."

Renie stopped in amazement, and Rufus Sebastain whistled softly.

CHAPTER VI.

" WHAT is the matter, Lucy ? Speak out."

" Yes, I will, because I feel certain Mr. Sebastain can keep his tongue still. That man, now in the house, is the man who had his aristocratic face flattened against the window in the drawing-room that night."

" Leopold Gunstan ; are you sure, Lucy ?"

" Quite ; it was Leopold Gunstan, and no other. I told you I should know him again, and I did the instant I saw his eyes. He is a queer gentleman ; for my part I had very much rather the north pole had him than

Ziegleheath. You two deem me mistaken, I suppose."

The two were considerably astonished and dubious, and Rufus Sebastain quickly told her so.

" It seems so strange, Miss Northwood, that he should act the spy, and at a relation's house too; don't you think you may be judging rashly ?"

" No I don't; and for two pins I would say it to his face, before anyone."

" No, no, Lucy," said Renie, " that is not allowable. Remember you cannot prove it, therefore you must not accuse him. Peace must be kept if possible."

" Well, I am sure Lady Rudkin will not be the one to make war," and Lucy laughed oddly.

There was a feeling of restraint on all three ; and as soon as possible Renie turned the conversation.

Meanwhile, how were things shaping them-

selves in-doors? In the surest possible form
to secure an invitation and friendliness.
The wanderer talked, and smoked large
cigars with Sir Bevis; while Lady Rudkin
prowled in and out of the room like a police-
man on duty.

Leopold Gunstan chatted to the old man,
and spoke of his past life; how he had roamed
about and seen pretty nearly everything, and
now thought of settling down. He got to
know all he wanted in a short space of time;
and that Rodney was the only child. Then
he spoke of Miss Rudkin, and Sir Bevis
quickly told him what a deal he thought of
dear Renie.

The cigar was not finished before the
Baronet had invited the stranger to stay at
Zeigleheath a week or more, and help at the
shooting.

"Well, thanks, Sir Bevis; I am partly
engaged to a friend some dozen miles from

Harley End; but I should like very much to stop here first."

" Well, then, do so; and I can send over for your things this afternoon, you need not go back at all; Lady Rudkin and the young ladies will take care of you."

" You are very good, I am sure."

And so it was settled. A man was dispatched in a dog cart to the " Crown and Thistle," at Harley End, for Mr. Gunstan's things; and during his absence that gentleman made himself at home, and smoked another cigar before luncheon.

The girls and Mr. Sebastain put in an appearance, and all seemed hungry, excepting my lady; she made great show, and ate little. Mr. Gunstan related to them some adventures as coolly as if he had been making a remark upon the weather, and Sir Bevis came to the conclusion, by the time the repast was ended, that he was an extremely nice fellow, and very gentlemanly. Something of this sort he said to Renie in the drawing-room, and she looked at the object of these remarks for a second. He was reclining on a couch by an open window, viewing the landscape with the eye of a connoisseur. The rest were not yet down; for once Renie was in good time.

As she listened to the kind old man talking by her side, and then glanced at the man by the window, a vague sort of terror seized her, and she turned and said abruptly—

" Uncle, tell me something about that man; what is he to us ?"

" Nothing in reality, Renie; the relationship goes for nothing. But he would have inherited these lands, had not Rodney been born, and will yet, if the child dies."

" Hush," said the girl, sharply, " don't speak of such a thing, uncle. Does he know it ?"

" Of course; has known it all his life. I wish Zeigleheath could descend to a female,

but it cannot; when the males are at an end
it goes to the Crown."

The old gentleman sighed, and looked round
the handsome room.

CHAPTER VII.

DINNER is over, and the drawing room empty
of all save Lady Rudkin. She stands before
the fire as if she were really cold, and every
now and then shivers. She looks remarkably
well in a bright brown silk dress, showing
her pretty white shoulders. The others are
in the studio, all but the wanderer; he is
roaming about, and has just had a friendly
chat with Christie Parnell in the corridor.
It is not at all astonishing that he bends his
steps to the drawing room; he is fond of his
ease. My lady does not hear him, she is

wrapt in her own reflections, so he stands and admires her with sleepy-looking eyes. Presently he moved to her side, and coolly said—

"Essy."

She wheeled round, her pretty hands held out, and her face glowing.

"Ah, Leo, I am—"

"There, there," and he put up his hand to keep her off, "don't get excited my dear girl. Of course you are glad to see me," and he laughed.

She looked at him beseechingly.

"Oh, Leo! are you angry?"

"No, not at all; but, Esther," and he bent his handsome face nearer, "this is a different meeting to our last. You have altered your position since then, and you did not ask my permission."

"But how could I know you were likely to find me?"

"Exactly. It did not seem probable, when you had flown so high, did it? But shall I

tell you something, Essy? I was the next
heir to this estate, failing your husband, the
old man, till *you* put a child's life in the way.
I have a good mind to make you squeeze the
breath out of that small body; I *could* make
you."

She recoiled in horror, and gasped—

"Leopold, for God's sake hush! How did
I know anything about what you were heir
to? you said you were poor."

"I was, but I am rich from to-day. I made
my fortune the night I looked at you through
that window. The biter's got bitten this
time, my lady; you should have had a little
more patience."

"Patience!" echoed she; "and had I not
patience? Have I ever done anything else
all my life but wait, till I was well nigh weary
of my own existence? Leo, could nothing
satisfy you but to come and torment me?
what is it you want?"

He laughed a low mocking laugh, and crossed his hands behind him.

"Gad! I don't know. Something that the laws of this country object to—a clean sweep. Essy, you know as well as I know that you don't care two straws for that proud old boy whose name you bear, and that you *do* care a good many for *me*. Now you are going to smart for your own happy contrivance; you have chained yourself, and I am free. The old man cannot last very long, and then think—you would have had the same position with a different husband. Don't you perceive your mistake?"

Lady Rudkin was white to the very lips; she knew what he said was true; his shot had hit the mark.

"Leopold, you are not generous; don't you see I suffer? It is your fault; you should have told me you were related to Sir Bevis."

"Should I? And then you would not have married him, eh? But you gave me no op-

portuuity, my lady (I must not forget to give
you your title, you are bound to pay for it).
You go and get married quietly, and I have
had some trouble to find your pretty nest.
Esther, I am going to stay here; are you not
charmed?"

"No, I am not; and you shall not stay, for
I will tell Sir Bevis."

This was only a flash in the pan, and so the
wanderer knew.

He laughed, and caressed his thick moustache.

"What a brave creature it is; if I were
you, I'd strike while the iron's hot. It is cold
now, positively. Look at me, Essy," and he
grasped her hand; "you are cold, but that
need not prevent you setting off to tell your
husband of my intention. Essy, look at me
—kiss me."

He suddenly caught her in his arms, and
pressed his lips to hers.

"Child, don't try to rouse the devil within

me; it only slumbers lightly. I have wandered all my life; am I to wander still? A chance of a home with you is gone, and I must stand aside, and let that baby lord it here. There," and he pushed her from him; "go and tell your husband."

"Leo, don't taunt me; it is too late now."

Tears were trickling down her fair cheeks. Leopold Gunstan saw them, and his mouth quivered.

"There is a great deal of the brute in me, Essy, is there not? It is well you can cry; I can't. But I am going to warm myself in the glow of prosperity a bit, Esther, so we had better be friends. The hostess is generally on good terms with her guests. Who is that Miss Rudkin?"

"Sir Bevis told you—his niece."

"She has money, I presume?"

"Ah! no; Renie is poor."

"For which you are not sorry, eh, Essy?" and he smiled. "It is a pity, because she is a rather nice sort; got a determined will, though. There is a bit of the 'dog in the manger' about you, Lady Rudkin; you have spoiled your own happiness, and you would like to spoil someone else's. But I imagine that to be a difficult task with Miss Rudkin; she is not to be upset easily."

My lady's face was clouded, and Leopold Gunstan had read it aright. It would have driven her mad to have seen the wanderer making love to Renie. A clatter of cups in the hall warned them of the approach of tea, and immediately they were masked as before, and discussing a general topic.

CHAPTER VIII.

IT was unusual for the drawing-room to be
so long deserted ; but there was a powerful
magnet at work, namely, Renie's pictures.

Sir Bevis had visited the studio, and Rufus
Sebastain, no longer able to contain himself,
blurted out to the bewildered baronet that
his niece Renie was an artist of no mean
repute.

Then came the confession of " My Pet "
in the Academy, and an exhibition of the
selection.

The old man was overjoyed, and clasped Renie to him again and again.

"I always said the little brown papoose was not an ordinary child, but I did not guess what you were so busy about. You have been as quiet as a mouse, my child, up in these dismal rooms."

"Oh, I am quite fond of them, uncle, and I think them quite cheerful, don't you, Lucy?"

That young lady nodded. It was rather a bone of contention between the two, those rooms in the west wing. Lucy considered that Renie ought to have two of the better ones, and not been put in those musty apartments. So, when appealed to, she declined to give any answer, further than a nod. Renie smiled, and Sir Bevis appeared rather uncomfortable, and asked again very earnestly—

"My dear child, are you *sure* you are comfortable and happy?"

"Yes; quite, uncle."

They were awakened out of their interesting discussion of Renie's pictures by a rap at the door, and upon Lucy opening it, a servant informed them my lady was waiting tea. It was a very merry going down stairs, and Leopold Gunstan, with the coolness which was his characteristic, inquired what had happened to clate them all so much.

No doubt Sir Bevis would have told, but that Renie whispered to him not. She had a strange aversion to the dark individual's knowing anything that concerned her. So he raised his eyebrows and smiled, as he sipped his tea—

"You are like your pet, Rodney, disposed to be antagonistic, Miss Rudkin. Well, it is, to say the least, ungenerous of you, for we do not stand on equal ground. I could not bring myself to contend with a lady, so I am vanquished."

"I think not, Mr. Gunstan; your eye tells a different tale."

"But I don't desire a feud with you; ours,

if once commenced, would, I fear, last as long as those of the Roses. So we won't begin."

"I have no mind to recognise right or feelings, where my sense points out to me the danger of gratifying either; so if I hurt your feelings by not telling you what you want to know, I cannot help it, and—I don't feel sorry."

"Then I am to understand from that that we are not friends, in short, engaged in a Christianlike warfare?"

"By no means; but I cannot say anything about future friendship, at present there certainly is none; I do not count my friends by the hour."

Leopold Gunstan set the cup down hastily.

"I beg your pardon, Miss Rudkin, I have presumed. But wanderers like myself are apt to make a home and friends at every stopping-place; it would not do for us to wait till we got home before we felt at home."

There was a slight pause after this, and my lady made an unusual clatter among the cups.

" Well done, Renie," said Lucy, later on, when Leopold Gunstan was detailing the mysteries of a buffalo hunt to Sir Bevis, Rufus, and Lady Rudkin, "you put that bean-stalk in his proper place splendidly. But he will keep a sharp eye on you in future."

" And he is welcome to, he will find mine as sharp."

The ill-feeling that existed between the French girl and Shepperton, increased rather than diminished as time went on, and one afternoon they went through a little violent exercise in the effervescence of their spirits. My lady had made a sweeping visit to the nurseries, and ordered Sedorice to make a little frock for Master Baby, and Shepperton was to bring her the material shortly. Not four seconds after she had gone, Master Baby made a pounce upon something on the floor, and fishing it up, cleverly waved

an envelope in the air. Sedorice took it
from him, but could not read the address;
and while she was sitting spelling the peculiar
letters out, Nurse Mary came into the room
and glanced over her shoulder. Before she
could do more than step on one side, Shepperton flounced in with her arms full of materials,
and began to instruct Sedorice as to their
purposes. But in the midst of this teaching
she came to a dead stand, with her eyes fixed
on Sedorice's knee. The things were dropped,
and her hand stretched out to grasp the
coveted object, only the French girl was too
sharp for her, and sprang aside, the French
temper burning in each cheek. Shepperton's
face presented a strong contrast to Sedorice's;
the one was in a temper, the other was
maddened by terror.

" Give me that, girl !" commanded the great
woman, following Sedorice round the room.

The girl was evidently bent upon mischief,
she curled her lips, snapped her fingers,

and shrugged her shoulders in Shepperton's face.

It was no use. Mrs. Shepperton commanded, Sedorice refused to obey. There was a grand rush, but Sedorice, now thoroughly roused, skipped about like a kitten, and set her at defiance. The only result of this farce was the overturning of a table and terrifying Rodney, who assisted at the uproar by howling most dismally, and catching at Sedorice's gown.

The noise reached Renie and Lucy; and Rufus Sebastain suggested that they should go and ascertain the cause.

They were not the only curious people; they met my lady hurrying to the scene of action.

"What *is* the matter?" asked Lady Rudkin, in the doorway.

The combatants came to a stop, and glared at each other; while Nurse Mary looked on with the child in her arms.

" My lady," commenced Shepperton, gasp-
ing for breath, " Sedorice has something of
mine which she will not give up ; it is of im-
portance to me, my lady. Will you tell her
to return it to me ?"

" It not your's ; it not. I let Mary see."

" No, no," screamed Shepperton, darting
forward, and barring the way. " My lady,
you look at it and decide whose it is."

Without a sound Lady Rudkin held out her
hand, and received from the girl a piece of
paper crumpled into a ball.

My lady opened it, and, looking at it,
replied slowly—

" Yes, Sedorice, this is Shepperton's," and
shut her hand on it like a vice.

It was only a scrap of paper, and yet Lady
Rudkin had turned as white as a ghost.
And she was not the only one. Nurse Mary
was perfectly colourless, and holding by a
chair.

" You cannot read well, I conclude,

Sedorice," remarked her mistress, smiling pleasantly, " or you would have discovered that this was an old letter of Shepperton's."

" No, miladi, I not make out well."

My lady laughed her pretty girlish giggle, and said—

" There, don't get fighting again ; and you, Shepperton, should be more careful than to carry your letters about."

Good advice; and since the letter really was Shepperton's, why did not my lady restore it to her instead of walking deliberately off with it ?

Shepperton speedily followed her mistress, and Sedorice rushed off to cool her ruffled temper.

She had not dared to contradict Lady Rudkin openly ; but her mouth clasped as if it required some little force to keep it shut.

Nurse Mary remained standing with little Rodney in her arms, his cheeks still wet.

" Mary, your sense of propriety is shocked, I see."

" That it is, Miss Renie; and more than that, too. No good comes of fighting, especially from such a cause."

" Well, never mind, my good Mary; Shepperton is imperious, and Sedorice headstrong and hot; the only wonder to me is that they have not had a passage of arms before."

" But you seem quite upset. Give me Rodney; are you faint?"

Certainly Mary looked as though she were.

" No, Miss Renie, thank you; I have only had a turn, and straightway she commenced to cry and gasp out between her sobs—

" I wish I had died before to-day, if this is how things are going to finish. May the Lord help us through it!"

" Nonsense, Mary; it is all over now; they won't quarrel again in a hurry. You will make this little fatty cry again. I had no idea you were so nervous."

"No, I am not nervous. Well, maybe, I am, and I guess I'll be worse; in fact, *all* of us, Miss Renie, before we're better."

With that Mary started up, and began an imaginary dusting.

The two girls eyed each other in astonishment, and Lucy said—

"Better leave her."

"Yes, come with me, Rodney, and I'll take care of you till Mary wants you."

The child readily agreed, and left the room.

Rufus Sebastain laughed heartily when he heard the cause of the disturbance, and told Rodney he was receiving scientific lessons early, that, what with French and sparring, he ought to make something out of the common.

CHAPTER IX.

"Lucy, what makes you so silent?" said Renie, when the girls were in their room for the night. We have no time to chatter, since Mr. Sebastain has been here — except at nights—and now you say nothing, but sit and admire the fender."

"I have changed places with you, Renie," replied Lucy, smiling, but still abstracted, "you used to be the silent one at school, and only opened your mouth to say a wise thing, like an Indian Chief."

"And this is, I suppose, a case of 'pass

the pipe ?' Well, to confess the truth, I was well occupied, following one of the studies of my early life, and over which I used to get into terrible disgrace. I was exercising my brain by means of that beneficial science, arithmetic, and had got as far only as the first rule, addition. I have spoken."

" So it would seem," laughed Renie, " but I cannot say I am much wiser for your speaking. What is the matter with you ?"

" Nothing is the matter with me; but there's something wrong with somebody else."

" Who is it ? and what is it?"

" I cannot tell you. I have not proved my sum yet; you disturbed me in the midst of my calculation. When the total is down you shall see it. But, Renie, I want you to tell me something in your dear, simple way, dearest. Who and what is Mr. Gunstan ? What makes him related to you ? and what does Sir Bevis know of him ?"

" Now, Lucy, you ask me more than I can

tell you; in short, as old James would say,
'you want to be fawst (fast).' But I asked
uncle about him, and what he told me rather
startled me, and made me uneasy, for what
earthly reason I have no idea. But I don't
like the man, in spite of his handsome face, I
distrust him, though I know no harm of him.
Leopold Gunstan (and Renie dropped her
voice slightly) is the next heir to Zeigleheath,
should little Rodney die. Uncle told me in
reality there is no relationship between him
and the Rudkins. His father's mother was a
second or third cousin of my great-grand-
father's; but it has worked round so that he
is the nearest male heir; a woman may not
inherit the lands, else there are Addy, myself,
and one or two female offshoots nearer than
this man. They never were on friendly terms,
but when this Leopold's father, who was an
awfully bad man, and in the army, died, the
widow began to write for small loans from
time to time, which of course were never

returned. However, nothing had been seen or heard of this Leopold till he wrote to uncle and then appeared."

" And where does his mother reside ?"

" His mother is now sixty, and lives in a poor way in a little Welsh village not far from Dolgelly. She has pinched herself all her life to let her son take things easy, and he appears to think she has done no more than her duty, in fact, owes him something for bringing him into the world where his boots were not to be laced with gold."

" But they will be, Renie, they will be. Let that man set his mind on anything, and he will get it. He is made of adamant."

There was a queer light in Lucy North-wood's eyes as she said this, and Renie, watching it, marvelled.

" Lucy, what is passing through your brain ?"

" A horrid fancy, a horrid fancy. And it is more than a fancy, it is almost a conviction. My sum is not, as I told you, finished, Renie,

when it is you shall see it. If I knew how to
get that man out of this house, I would not
be long doing it. Renie, as surely as we two
are sitting here, so surely will Leopold Gunstan bring harm and sorrow to Zeigleheath.
It was he I saw looking in at the window,
though you and Mr. Sebastain don't believe
it, but it was. I have kept my eyes open
since, and it has not been for nothing."

"Lucy, you make me sick with terror,
what is it you fear? You are worse than
Mrs. Troost and nurse!"

"Am I? well, they are not far short of the
mark; depend upon it they are not fools. It
is strange your suspicions have not been
aroused!"

"No, they have not, and I don't imagine
they will. I don't care to root out a why and
a wherefore for every action and speech; let
things take their chance, I am no fit person
to meddle. And I'll tell you what it is, Lucy,
I firmly believe that people who are everlast-

ingly hunting for something, generally find it, and too often something unpleasant. Now, I don't want to be a finder, especially in this house; if there's anything wrong let it stay, a loose thing frequently hangs together a long time, and I have patience to wait till it shall part of its own accord."

Lucy smiled and kissed her friend.

"Not changed one atom, Renie, ready to give everyone a chance. I don't believe if you saw a murder committed that you would go and convict the murderer!"

"I certainly should not like to swear any-one's life away, Lucy, and I hope I shall never be put in such an awful position. Yet I trust I should not fail in my duty, whatever it might be."

"You and I are suitable friends, Renie. You have courage and determination, I have curiosity and suspicion. I shall discover, you shall act; that being settled, we'll get into bed."

One day it suddenly occurred to Renie that they had not behaved quite politely to the Count and Countess; they had never been for that roving afternoon which the good-natured Carl had asked them to go for, and to which they had assented. When Renie proposed that it should be delayed no longer, Lucy and the pleasure-loving artist made no demur, and they proceeded to dress. But barely had Renie put on her hat before a step sounded in the corridor, and a voice called—

" Renie, my dear !"

" Quick, Renie ; that's Sir Bevis."

And so it was. He was standing in the studio window, and seemed disappointed when the girls appeared, dressed for walking.

" Going out, my love ?"

" Yes, uncle, I thought of doing so ; but if you will sit with me, I should like that infinitely better. Lucy, you and Mr. Sebastain must take care of each other, and remember me to the Count and Countess."

Lucy complied; and the Baronet made no
attempt to prevent Renie stopping, so she
tossed off her bonnet, and sat down. Her
quick eye had detected a change in the old
man; she saw something was a trouble. He
had not been looking at all well lately, and as
he stood gazing out over the sea, she noticed
how haggard and aged he appeared. And the
change had not been gradual, it had come
suddenly. She did not like to question him,
and he was silent. She wondered how long
he would stand looking so sad and lonely,
with the sun shining in a lurid glow over his
head, and turning the white locks to fire.

The sea was heaving its bosom with a
gentle swell, and rocked the returning fishing
boats as gently as a mother would the cradle
of her first-born. Such sounds as the lowing
of cattle, the barking of dogs, and the cry of
the sea birds as they dipped into the clear,
green waters, found their way into the room,
and yet Sir Bevis stood wrapt in thought,

which seemed all sorrow. There was no gleam of hope, no flash of light across the chiselled face; it was so set, so stony, in its despair, that Renie grew afraid, and feared lest the spirit should pass away ¦with that solemn hush.

She touched his hand, and drew back; it was so cold, so like the hand of death.

"Uncle, have you nothing to say to me?"

His eyes slowly sought her face, and studied it attentively for several seconds. Then a faint smile crossed the wan face, and he said—

"Yes, Renie, much."

He was now fairly aroused, and looked round.

"Is that room empty? Go and see, and secure the doors. I want to talk to you."

Renie obeyed, wondering as she went.

"Yes, they are fast; and we are alone, uncle."

"Then sit down close to me, child, and listen."

Renie selected a sewing chair near the casement, and leaning her arm on the window-seat, prepared herself to attend. But though all was ready, Sir Bevis seemed loth to begin, and half inclined to drift into the old dream out of which Renie had just roused him. Suddenly he started, and said—

"Renie, you have not forgotten my last conversation alone with you?"

"No, uncle."

"I am glad of that, dear child, because I need not repeat it. When I asked you to protect my child then, I had no idea what sort of a request I was making, or the urgent need of it. But I know you are strong where many are weak, Renie; I know that you are not easily daunted or turned by the opinion of others. You asked me for time to consider the matter before giving me your final answer. You have had time; what is your decision?"

"I agree to take the trust, and I will always do my best for your boy."

The old man clasped his hands thankfully.

"God bless you, Renie, God bless you. You have robbed me of half my bitterness. And now listen. Since you are his guardian it is only fair that I should be candid with you. You are a true Rudkin, Renie, proud and reserved; you have suffered, and will suffer, for my foolishness. I should not have married; I see my mistake plainly now. I have forced you to work and sobered your young life. And that work must, I fear, be continued, for I have little to leave you now, and you are not cut out for a pauper. And now I give into your keeping a child, as if you had not enough to take care of yourself. But I am driven to it, Renie, by sheer necessity. I repose confidence in you, and it is no easy charge. I dare not leave Rodney to the care of a thoughtless person. Renie, you must never let the child away from you; he must not go out of the house you live in for one night to his mother or any of her friends;

he must never, if possible, be with anyone but those you can trust as yourself. I know you are quick at discernment, use your own judgment in all things. I leave you full power, sole guardian of Rodney Bevis, with Norman Howard to aid you when you require help. Remember, his mother has no earthly claim, no control over him; he is your child, and I charge you to take him wherever you go. His income will be good, and it is in your hands till he comes of age, then he manages his own affairs, subject to your guidance. The income of Lady Rudkin is a distinct thing, and she can go and enjoy it at Jerusalem if she likes. You are the mistress of Zeigleheath. Franklin Chalmers, of Friars' Inn, is my lawyer; he is the son of George Chalmers, and a young man, so that in all probability you can carry on the estate together for years. He is coming down in the morning, and I want you to see him, but he will be in my rooms, and his name will not transpire."

A sigh of relief, and the old gentleman leant back in his chair. During this code of instructions Renie's face had got blanched, and now she spake in a low, horrified tone.

"Uncle, for Heaven's sake tell me what is the matter that you have left your affairs so strangely, and why tell me of them now?"

"Because there is no time like the present, Renie, and I have received my death blow."

"Oh, uncle, what is it?"

"No, my dear girl, no, I will not tell, I will not betray my heart's misery. I will be brave, and the grave shall not receive a traitor and a coward. I have been punished, Renie, for my folly; I have made a mistake."

"Uncle," said Renie, bending near the old man, "why did you marry her?"

He started.

"Oh! Renie, I was a fool to try and hood-wink *you*; and I did it against my conscience, because I *saw* your eyes were opened at the beginning. But you have behaved well, child, and I thank you for your delicacy. Not by word or look have you betrayed your discovery all this time. I know your opinion, though. Ah, well ! You asked me that question once before Renie, why did I do so and so." He seemed to shirk the words. "I did it because I verily believe I was mad at that time ; I must have been. And I fancy it was as much pity for her youth and beauty as anything else. I found her at an hotel at Brighton ; she was acting as companion and upper lady's maid to a vulgar, exacting woman with a double chin, and her pretty, affectionate ways and sorrowful story touched my heart. She told me she was an orphan, alone in the world, that her father had been a minister, and died of some epidemic caught while ministering to his flock on their beds of sickness. She seemed so young, so affectionate to be friendless and alone in the world, that I, in a moment of weakness at seeing her crying, offered her my protection, and, like an

old fool, mistook her sweetness and gentle
gladness to be for love of me, instead of
delight at the position I held out to her, which
it assuredly was. It was no sooner arranged
than done, and we were married quietly at St.
James's, on the beach. She wrote to one relation, a Mrs. Lofgan, her aunt, and with
whom she had been living since her father's
death, but that lady could not be present at
the wedding on account of her school of little
boys. When I brought her home, the dis-
mayed looks of Norman and Addy and the
old servants caused me to think that I had
made a mistake to marry at my age, and so I
had."

"But, uncle, why did you not marry before
when you were young?"

A look of inexpressible sadness crossed the
Baronet's face, and something very like a tear
hung to the long lashes.

"Renie, it is good sometimes to hear a true
story, a lesson from the lips of one who has

learnt it. You have been kept in the dark
with respect to your family ; not because there
is any disgrace attached to them, but because
they are always attended with some misfortune. There is a curse on the Rudkins,
Renie, and that curse is a fair woman.
One out of every generation has married a
fair woman, and each time there has been a
fresh misfortune. I am the one this time to
revive it, old as I am ; Rodney may, perhaps,
escape it, but if he has children surely one
will marry a blonde. I suppose it will last as
long as the Rudkins. Renie, I had my love
years ago, and—I lost her. That is why I
never married, and I have only married now
to carry out the curse, it seems, not for
love."

"Did the lady die, uncle?"

"Renie, I will tell you what I have never
told to mortal, and it is a lifetime since it
happened. When I was a young man I went
to see your father at Chichester, and there

was a ball given by the officers. I was
present, so was a little creature with soft
curls, and as timid and light as a fairy. Her
hair clustered in nut brown rings round her
white forehead. We found a deal to say to
each other, and we found out we loved each
other before that ball came to an end. She
looked so sad, so pleading, as I gave her into
her mother's keeping, that I was puzzled.
But I had not long to puzzle. Renie, I had
fallen in love with another man's wife. The
little creature was the wife of the doctor of
the regiment, they had been married two
months. We met often, for we were like
gnats flying round a lamp, we could not resist
the light, and we loved each other—oh God!
so truly. What a horrible realisation it was
that we were parted for ever! and what en-
hanced the bitterness was that Amy had not
really loved her husband, the marriage had
been arranged by Mrs. Arden. Amy had no
fortune, and her mother's income was small.

"We parted with the understanding that we were never to see each other again; to be strangers for ever more. And I came back here a crushed man; a stranger, too truly, to all happiness. I have often wondered why God let it happen. In the following December, I was one night sitting in my study, smoking, when I fell into a queer state—partly a doze, partly a reverie—and my love's angel spirit came to me out of a ray of light, and twined her arms round my neck, and kissed me. I felt the pressure of those soft lips warm on my own; it was like the only kiss we had ever taken when we said good-bye—a long, lingering kiss. She said, in tones wonderfully low and sweet—

"'Bevis, I am going home; don't forget me.'

"Then the light covered her, and hid her from my sight; and I was alone, yearning for one more kiss.

"I jumped up, and glanced at the clock;

it was midnight, and the snow falling thickly; it was the first fall that winter.

"In a day or two I made a journey down to the place where Doctor Nash was stationed. I found him with crape nearly to the top of his hat. Amy had gone home, as she told me that night, and left a little baby behind her. And I knew my love had been with me; I knew that God had let her come all radiant with His glory to say a parting word to me; to comfort me before she was taken out of my sight for all these weary years. Ah, my heart's darling! are you tired of watching? Have I been so *very* long? But there's only a little bit longer, dear one; only a little bit. I am coming now."

The far-off look had come to the old man's face again, and he had forgotten Renie and everything else; but sat, with his hands shading his eyes, watching for his dear one over the sunlit sea. Aye, he had spoken truly—it *was* only a little bit; for he was already drifting across that golden sea to the haven of rest; there to be moored for evermore alongside of his heart's darling!

Tears were rolling down Renie's pale cheeks as she kissed the withered hand.

"What, crying, Renie!" exclaimed the old man, bowing his white head to hers; "don't weep for me, dear child. But now you know what has made my life so cold and stony; my heart passed through the mill years ago. I have trusted you with my secret, as I trust you with my boy, for I *know* both are safe with you, poor Denis's brown baby."

"Don't look at me so sadly, dear uncle; I will mind all you have told me, and be faithful to Rodney."

Sir Bevis smiled, and stroked her head fondly.

"I will go now, my dear; we shall meet again at dinner."

"Yes, uncle."

Twilight had deepened, and Renie guided

him to the door, and watched him along the
dark corridor ; then shut herself in, and, sink-
ing on her knees by the window, she asked
God to help her with this fresh burthen, and
enable her to discharge her duty faithfully.
She might well ask for aid ; it was a hard
task to undertake almost single-handed ; and
Renie wished, as she kneeled there, that the
child had no fortune ; his money was a great
anxiety to her.

CHAPTER X.

In the midst of Renie's grave meditation, Lucy entered, her cheeks glowing with the keen air, for it now blew fresh from the sea in an evening.

"Oh, Renie, I wish you had been with us, it has been so nice. Only the stuffed animals frightened me awfully at first. When the door opens you are confronted by a huge bear, with its arms open to embrace you. And at one corner of the garden there resides a kangaroo, and the Countess told me that one day the creature got away, and they had

such a chase after it, quite a kangaroo hunt
in the village. Imagine how 'Croquet' would
frisk about, to the detriment of the Moordart
maidens' hearts, and exclaim ' By Jingo!'
and ' I beg your pardon,' in one breath.

Renie let Lucy chatter on; it sounded
rather queer to her at times, for she had Sir
Bevis and Rodney running in her head, but
she said nothing in return, and this Lucy was
quick to perceive.

" My gracious, Renie ! What's to do ? Have
you been chief mourner at a funeral during
my absence ? Is your mouth stitched up,
like Dick's ferret's sometimes, that you
neither speak nor laugh ?"

" No, Lucy, my mouth's all right but my
heart's not, and I think that's worse."

" Undoubtedly; and what's amiss with that
important organ ? Have you fallen in love
with Mr. Gunstan this afternoon, for want of
something better to do ?"

" No, that I have not. Lucy, dear, don't

tease me ; I feel so restless this evening and
am compelled to be silent lest I say what I
ought not.   Did the Countess ask after me ?"

"Oh dear yes, and went into quite a
transport about you to Mr. Sebastain, who
bowed every now and then, and fidgetted as
if the sofa were hot.   However, they fortunately both came to one conclusion at the
same moment—that you were a decidedly
superior sort of young lady, with far more
sense than generally falls to the lot of us poor
wavering mortals.   I sat by, and felt myself
gradually getting less and less; indeed, had
not the good-natured Count come to my
rescue, I doubt if there would have been
any of me left to present to your superior
majesty."

" I suppose the good-natured Count soothed
your feelings by making love to you, eh,
Lucy ?"

" No, I can't say that he did, though he did
walk back with us, and looked very *distingué*

in a dark green top coat with fur collar and cuffs. He certainly is not half a bad fellow, Renie, and I am not very sure but that if he asked me I'd say ' yes,' instead of ' ask mamma,' as a proper young damsel ought to do. Mr. Sebastain has been in the dumps this afternoon."

" Has he? What's wrong, I wonder?"

" Be at rest; he'll tell you, with his cherub face as sad as sad. Renie, don't you go and mistake the cards you hold in your hands. Platonic friendship appears to me to be a rather dangerous game to play at with a good-looking young man like Rufus Sebastain."

" My *dear* Lucy! what will you say next? Surely I can be on friendly terms with a gentleman without falling in love with him."

" Yes, I daresay *you* can; but how about him?"

And Miss Northwood gave her pretty head a sagacious shake. The conversation stopped there, not so the train of thought it had

awakened, and Renie, honest and straight-
forward as ever, did not try to stay them,
but took her heart to task. It was a curious
examination that, and affairs were found to
be in a very bewildered condition, so much
so that Renie too got confused and, jumbling
them all in again, shut the door. And this
young girl is not the only one that has done
it. It requires a fair amount of moral
courage to turn one's heart inside out and
examine the contents ; and a great many
people walk round, but never look inside, like
valiant policemen when they see a light in a
house at an unusual hour.

Renie began to think about her life; it had
always been clouded, and just now the clouds
seemed blacker than ever. She wondered if
the sun was never going to rise for her as it
did for other young girls ; if she was never
to have a home, and be free to rest ?
" Never !" replied her conscience, " till you

have secured to yourself an independence, enough to make a little home for yourself."

That evening was quiet; Sir Bevis and Renie often caught themselves looking at each other in a sad, wistful way. The only one that appeared free from thought or care was Leopold Gunstan.

Amongst his wiles and arts was music. Where he had learnt there was no telling, but no doubt his poor weak loving mother drew her tether still tighter to allow her lamb more play, and had had him taught music. And his talent was by no means to be scoffed at; he possessed an excellent ear, and could play anything. Amongst his varied collection was an Indian war dance, the tune, if so it can be called, the savages sing when their victims are roasting. It was a series of the most complicated and horrible sounds, and set every nerve in your body quivering.

How Leopold Gunstan managed to play it

was a wonder, but he did, and most effectively, too.

" Where did you learn that, Mr. Gunstan?" asked Lucy.

" That is the war song of the Black-foot Indians. I stayed in their camp some time with a party of hunters, and I might have married the chief's daughter, ' Starlight,' only I funked it at the last when I thought of England."

He laughed, and related what she was like, and the strings of beads she presented him with.

" Once she stuffed into my pocket a charm that was to preserve me healthy and whole for ever, and ensure me a safe pass to the happy hunting ground when the Great Spirit spat fire at me ; and when I took the precious relic out of my pocket I found it was a baby's foot, not quite cold."

He went off into another roar of laughter, till the music-stool creaked again under his weight.

" For goodness sake stop, Gunstan !" exclaimed Rufus Sebastain ; " you make me quite sick !"

" Nonsense, my dear fellow ! You should be their guest for a bit, and you'd soon get over the faintness !"

" Heaven forbid !" ejaculated the artist. " I don't want to become a savage !"

CHAPTER XI.

THE next morning Frost knocked at the door of the studio, about half-past eleven, and told Miss Renie Sir Bevis wished to speak to her in his study.

Renie rightly guessed what it was, and at once obeyed the call.

She was correct; Mr. Franklin Chalmers had arrived, and sat talking to her uncle. He was a man of thirty-three or four—not much, if any, more—with a bald head, a fringe of dark hair round, and a moustache to corres-pond. His face was just as pleasant as a face could be, and with a faint rose colour in his cheeks which showed off his deeply-set eyes.

There was a bashful bluntness in his manner, and he persisted in keeping his mouth as much shut as possible when speaking.

His shoulders were broad enough for a bigger man, and rather inclined to be high. But Renie took a fancy to him and formed her opinion of him, that he was frank, good-natured, kind hearted and blunt; not over fond of himself, and, therefore, disposed to be merciful and charitable to others.

And this man her uncle had selected to be her adviser and assistant in the coming struggle. Good. Renie was well pleased with his choice. Mr. Chalmers left before luncheon, and Troost let him out as she had let him in.

The nights were now excessively cold, and fires were the order of the day at Zeiglcheath after five o'clock. Sir Bevis cowered over

one all day in his own room, and sat close by
it in the drawing-room. His explanation for
it was that he had got a chill, followed by a
deep sigh and a glance at Renie. But the
sharp air did not drive the gipsies away, they
remained by the old mill, and had appro-
priated the rooms in it in addition to their
vans and tents. Apparently they had settled
for the winter.

Neither of the visitants to the camp had
disclosed the fortune predicted for them by
the hag; but Lucy promised Renie that she
should hear her's as soon as the given time
had expired. Mostly now in the evenings
Leopold Gunstan absented himself. He was
quite at home, and acted like one of the
family, and no one gave a thought to his
rambles. Sometimes the girls accompanied
Rufus Sebastain on to the terrace, when he
smoked, and it was natural a wandering man
should stroll about.

He frequently told them what a walker he

was, so that, when missed, it would be—
" Oh, he is taking some long walk."

The first who gained any knowledge of the
direction Mr. Gunstan's wanderings took was
pretty Christie Parnell.

" Mr. Gunstan does not stretch his legs
over much, Miss Renie," said her handmaiden
one evening, while on her knees blowing the
fire, which was not red enough to suit her
fancy.

" Yes, I think he does; he walks mostly in
the evenings now, Christie."

" But only as far as the river side, Miss
Renie."

" How do you know that pray? He went
to the post to see if they had a paper stating
the time the San Francisco mail goes out last
night."

" *That* he never did, Miss Renie; that's a
fib, if ever there was one. Because I was
there buying myself some dresses and aprons
till the shop shut, and Mrs. Magnet would

have told me if he had been before ; besides that was impossible, for I did not go till dinner was over. But I'll tell you where he *did* go, and that's to the river side. Robert Barnett was so polite as to bring me home last night, in case I might feel lonesome, and we came the longest way. Robert said it was a quieter road round by the mill wood. Well, Miss Renie, when we got to the bank hard by the bridge, I sees a tall figure standing by the coppice gate, and I turned all of a tremble, thinking it might be one of them wild gipsy fellows. But, as Mr. Barnett was with me, I took heart, Miss Renie, and walked on, shaking like a haspen leaf; and when we was passed I looked round and I saw by the moonlight Mr. Gunstan's face. Maybe he went to get his fortune told."

" Possibly," replied Renie, slowly ; while Lucy gave a significant ahem.

" I'll bet you fifty pounds to a hay seed, as Mr. Howard would say, that Christie's right, and that Mr. Gunstan was by the coppice gate last night, Renie; though he came in and said that he only went about the San Francisco mail. Every second word that man utters is a falsehood. Depend upon it Christie's mind is made up that it was he, or she would have taken more trouble to convince you."

Lucy's remark was a just one. Christie had no sooner finished her recitation than she left the room, as if she had no doubts herself, and that it was next to impossible that any-one else could have any. Renie took a little time before answering Lucy, then said—

"Well, allowing it was Mr. Gunstan, what need to come in and tell such a deliberate story, for it was of no moment to any of us whether he had been to the coppice gate or the Post Office?"

"Ah! there *was* need of the lie, be sure of that, my dear; Leopold Gunstan never does or says anything without a purpose. Renie, that man is as false as he is crafty; he is

wearing a mask in this house, acting a part—
I feel convinced of it. If I am judging him
wrongly, may God forgive me."

"Lucy, you denounced him at once, and
have since kept repeating your dismal fore-
bodings. You make me terrified, for I cannot
hide from either you or myself any longer
that I share them. I am almost stifled at times
with a sense, a feeling, of approaching danger
and oppression, from what direction I cannot
tell.   And yet when I come to examine my
fears, they are mere shadows, they assume no
decided form, and seem entirely groundless.
If I knew anything to make use of against
the man, I would tell uncle.   There is only
your assertion, that it was he at the window
that night, and *that* you cannot prove."

"True; and one should not make an accu-
sation without having proof; moreover, if we
did tell Sir Bevis, it would be no easy matter
to explain our fears to him, and in all probability he would laugh at us for our pains."

It was a pity the knotted coppice gate could not have spoken, or that Christie Parnell had not eyes and ears behind her. She and her brave swain had not long been out of sight before the figure by the gate began to evince symptoms of irritation, and at last came out with a good round oath, and commenced whistling softly to himself " The Gipsy Countess."

" Hang it all! it's deuced cold. I wonder if that black-eyed Susan's ever coming. This comes of residing with a set of aristocratic innocents who don't gamble, who don't bet, who do nothing. One *must* have some amusement in this stagnant hole, so I am fain to take the best that offers in the cool of an October night. And she *is* an uncommonly pretty little darling, this child of the woods, and believes every word you say to be gospel. She is not very exacting either; a kiss goes a long way with her, and she studies my profile with love lit eyes, while I am working

G 2

out a problem that would rather astonish her weak mind if explained to her," and the speaker laughed complacently, and the strong white fangs glittered in the moonlight.

He was beginning to soliloquise once more, when a light foot-fall broke upon his acute ear, and, turning round, he clasped a form in his arm, and exclaimed, fondly—

"My angel, you are here at last! I was almost distracted lest anything should have happened to you, dear one."

Althea (for it was the gipsy princess) laughed a wild, musical laugh, and clapped her pretty little hands with delight.

"So you were unhappy about me? I am so glad."

"Glad?"

"Yes, because, oh, Leopold, I sometimes fear you will cease to care for Althea, talking to all the ladies who go to the big house."

The beautiful eyes were brimful of sadness and tears, as they gazed into the wanderer's face. He had rarely, in all his rambles, seen a more lovely face than this one, and there was a particle of truth in his voice as he said—

"Don't be unhappy, my pet; there are none of them as sweet as you, my wild bird. Some of them are fair—

> "'But what care I how fair she be,
> If she be not fair to me.'

I have only eyes for you, Althea; and what have you got to say to me to-night?"

"Only the old thing—I love you."

That was Althea's song, "I love you;" and Leopold Gunstan liked it well enough; indeed, too well, for he made her repeat it many times.

"Are you sure, Althea?"

"Sure that I *love* you? Ah, yes, quite sure."

Then, clasping her hands, she went on vehemently, as if afraid he would doubt her—

"I love you for yourself, whether you are rich or poor; I love you now, I shall love you ever. Tell me if you don't love me, but don't let me lose you; I would sooner die."

The devil speaks and smiles.

" Althea, I do love you; but I am not rich, that is to say, I am poor."

" Ah, that is better still."

" Why so ?"

" Because it brings you nearer to me, Leo-pold; I am poor. You are a gentleman; you look fit to be a nobleman; and I am only a gipsy girl, though I am a princess. Our people call me Princess Althea. But I sup-pose that is not much."

Leopold laughed.

" No, not much anywhere, except amongst your tribe in the woods, dearest. I don't think I must take you away from them, eh?"

" I should be sorry; I sometimes think I could not live in the towns we pass through; but I'd try with you, Leopold, dear. But couldn't you come to our home? it is so beautiful living in the woods."

"You engaging child;" and he patted one round cheek. "I don't fancy a woodland life would agree with my constitution, Althea."

"What is that, Leopold?"

He laughed.

"That's a long word for you; but you are a capital pupil, and pick up amazingly. Never mind what it is, my dear; rest content, I shall not take you from your greenwood home at present, or—"

The conclusion of the sentence was too low for Althea's ears.

"See," continued the handsome *roué*, "I have brought you a little offering, my princess;" and he held out to her a lovely camellia of deep red tint, with a green leaf and bud. No need to ask where he got it; it came from the hot-house at Zeigleheath, and the head gardener would be wild in the morning at the loss of it.

"Ah, how lovely," said the girl, handling

it tenderly, and kissing it.   "How beautiful;
isn't it, Leopold?"

"I suppose so, my dear; and now you had
better go back to your kingdom, princess.
Are you cold?"

"No, not a bit;" and she pulled her scarlet
wrap closer round her.   "Are you?"

"Awfully.   These meetings can't take
place very often while this sharp weather
lasts."

It was by no means a lover-like speech.
But Althea only felt pity for her lord and
master's coldness, and actually said so to the
selfish man.   Love blinded her beautiful eyes.
He was a very god to her innocent heart.

"Never mind; run off, dear."

She put up her lovely face for a kiss, and
he condescendingly gave her one, and she fled
back to the camp like a startled fawn.

He stood and watched her for a minute, and
then went walking down the river side mur-
muring—

" You're a fool, Leopold Gunstan ! A fool!
You're always getting your wings clipped.
But this princess is not such a bad spec as the
savage one, oh, no !" and he began to laugh
heartily.

Presently he lighted a cigar, and stood on
the bridge by the island gazing on the moon-
lit lands with a hard look.

" Only a child between me and you," said
he, looking round, " only a feeble child."

CHAPTER XII.

" Renie," said Sir Bevis, one morning, " come with me, dear !"

She did so, and in the study he put a letter into her hand, saying—

" Read it."

It ran thus:—

> " Fellbrook, October 12th.
>
> "Dear Cousin Bevis,—
>
> " In answer to your kind letter I can only say I shall be charmed to pay you a visit. I heard of your remarkable marriage, and hope everything is bright in that direction.

I have seen some of the ups and downs of life, but still manage to keep comfortable, and have a good old-fashioned wardrobe with care. I fancy I am a little agitated to-day—quite an unusual thing for me, cousin—so will, therefore, postpone any further remarks till Thursday, when I hope to behold with my eyes the considerate Cousin Bevis I now address with my pen.

" Peaceful amid many vicissitudes is

" PRISCILLA TRUFIT."

" Uncle, who is this ?" exclaimed Renie, in astonishment, when she arrived at the end of this odd epistle.

" That lady is what she says, a cousin of mine, but nothing to you. Hers has not been a happy life, Renie ; she met cares and troubles young like—like *you*, my child, only she was not so able to combat them as you are, poor creature ! Her father was a very clever man—a professor of chemistry at one of

the Universities—but he died at an early age
and left the two daughters, Priscilla being the
eldest. The younger married a poor curate,
and went to Jamacia with him, where they
both died. They were always needy, for her
father was extravagant, so that Priscilla has
lived with an old maid as some sort of companion and friend, and saved her money, or,
at any rate, made it go further. In glancing
over my papers the other day I found some
letters of hers, and it struck me it might be a
kindness to her to be acquainted with you,
Renie; and I invited her to come on a visit.
She is the only old relative (if I may call it
such) that you have, my dear; and when anything happens, and you have this place and
the boy on your hands, Priscilla might be a
slight help to you on account of her age. If
you liked her you might give her house room,
Renie. But that, of course, is your own
affair."

Renie listened quietly, and then replied—

" Yes, I understand what you mean, uncle.
I daresay I should feel lost here by myself.
And then I could not have any gentlemen to
see me; and Mr. Sebastain I should not like
to cast away."

" No, certainly not, my dear; a very
proper thought. He is a nice young man,
and clever; don't lose sight of him, Renie:
there is something in his face I like exceed-
ingly. So that the presence of Priscilla
would do away with any obstacle, and you
could invite anyone you liked. I am glad I
thought of it."

As Renie left the room, the idea struck her
forcibly that all Sir Bevis' plans bore no re-
ference to his wife, she seemed to have passed
from his mind of late. He had actually pro-
vided an elderly lady to keep Renie in countenance when she chose to invite people.
Clearly Lady Rudkin was not to be present.
What was to become of her and her jointure ?

By the three train on the Thursday Miss

Trufit was to arrive, and the carriage was sent to meet her.

While it is on its way home, let us fly and take a peep at its occupant.

Miss Priscilla Trufit is sitting upright, and rigid, not because she is frozen internally and externally, but from force of habit. Miss Somerville, the rich old maid she has lived with, sits so, and Miss Trufit, being her companion, must follow her example. It is rather soon for her to have realized that she is not hired, that she is out of bondage, and free to crook her spare back if she likes. Very spare is Miss Priscilla, and very pretty, but eccentric to the last degree. She sits, as I have just said, very upright, looking at the men's backs, but though the mouth is nipped into a thin curve, it is not a hard mouth; indeed there is nothing hard or strong minded about the thin pale face, with its two bunches of white ringlets looped up with tortoiseshell combs. The professor's daughter was natu-

rally a weak woman, and her principal weak-
nesses were family and dress. She would
rather have been what she was, a gentlewoman
and poor, than an upstart and rich. Her
vanity was lasting, but weak; she chose
subdued finery, black and gray, and delicate
laces, relics of her mother's, who was of high
family. But her ideas on that subject, like
every other, were few. Her ideas about dress
never extended further than a ruche and a
marabow feather; beyond these two things
she could not get, and if her dressmaker had
not supplied the deficiency, Miss Priscilla
would, ten chances to one, have gone
skirtless.

She could not call up new ideas, any more
than she could new fashions and manners.
She always did the same thing on the same
occasions, and always had done. She carried
the same little black velvet bag on her arm,
filled with smelling salts, lavender, and her
purse, that she did twenty years ago, and the

same umbrella, with the immense white (now yellow) ivory button on the top. Her dinner dresses were all much the same cut and colours, black, lavender, and grey, her head dress black or white lace lappets, pinned with a diamond star. She was a small person, and of feathery weight. Her meditations, whatever they were, had not come to an end when the carriage stopped at the door.

Miss Priscilla gave a little flutter, like a poor timid bird, righted herself, grasped her umbrella, and prepared to alight.

Lady Rudkin thought to reassure her by her kind patronage, but Miss Trufit made my lady a graceful bend like the introduction to the *minuet de la cour*, which so petrified her that she beat a retreat and left Sir Bevis and Renie to proceed with the antics.

" And who is this, Cousin Bevis ?"

" This is Renie Dorothy, Denis's baby. You remember, Priscilla, there were two, Adeline and an infant ?"

" Yes, perfectly, Cousin Bevis, and this is the infant, poor thing. My dear, take my bag and umbrella, while I look at you ?"

Renie received the precious articles, and the little old lady drew out of the bosom of her shawl a massive gold eye glass, and adjusting it, surveyed the infant.

" Ah ! a true Rudkin, a true Rudkin ! Kiss me, my dear ?"

Renie kissed the delicate face, and half smiled at her uncle.

" I will now relieve you of those things, my dear ; I—why, bless us all, what's *this* ?"

The sight that had so terrified Miss Trufit was none other than Master Baby riding down the hall astride on his papa's gold-headed stick. Lucy Northwood had been so obliging as to fix a tail of rags to the extremity of it, and Rodney, nothing daunted, came prancing along on it. Miss Priscilla regarded him steadily through the eye-glass, and at last proclaimed, in measured tones—

" That is your boy, Cousin Bevis !   Well, I
would not allow him to play at that game,
whatever it is.   It will produce ossification of
the spine ; no, that is not right.   That is
caused by sitting very long on something too
hard.   But I am convinced this will produce
something, Cousin Bevis."

Sir Bevis and Renie laughed, and Rodney
came frisking round like the clown at a
Pantomime Review to inspect the new comer.

" Come and speak to Miss Trufit, Rodney,"
said his father.

" Miss Youfit," repeated the baby, approaching her, and stopping his fiery steed.

" Yes—Miss Trufit.   Won't you kiss me,
love ?"

The old lady's tone was gentle enough to
have tempted a more perverse child than little
Rodney, and he at once lifted his pretty face,
and while she kissed him clutched at one
bunch of white curls, and pronounced it to be
" Very pitty."

Miss Trufit looked long at the child, and then said—

" Like his mother ?"

" Yes," replied Sir Bevis, " in complexion and hair."

Miss Priscilla asked Renie to go with her to her room.

" I feel strange in this great place, my dear ; we old people cannot get accustomed to novelties so quickly as young ones. Don't go, Renie ; sit with me for a few moments," and Miss Trufit sank on the sofa.

Presently she began again—

" It is queer, me coming to Zeiglehealth. I was once here when a child ; I am four years older than Cousin Bevis, and I came with my mother. I thought it such a grand place, and got terrified by the long corri- dors. I never thought to see it again. But Cousin Bevis wished it very much, and it seems like coming home. I see him greatly changed, though, my dear; and that young wife—how pretty she is! but *what* a child."

"Yes," responded Renie, feeling she was expected to say something; "Lady Rudkin is both pretty and youthful."

"How do you get along with her?" inquired the sharp Miss Trufit.

Renie hesitated how to frame her reply.

"Well, I never by any means do anything I think likely to bring us into five minutes' conversation, so I have never clashed with her."

"That's prudent of you, child," said the old lady, "for I see plainly that you two would not get along at all peaceably. You are the image of Lady Dorothy; she was cousin to my mother. That is how the line is drawn, and your uncle has never allowed it, faint as it is, to become extinct. Are you rich, Renie?"

"No, Miss Trufit, I am not," and Renie smiled.

" Ah, is that so ? Sorry to hear it ; sorry, very. My dear, take an old woman's advice, try and do something for yourself to swell your income while you are *young*. You will never miss the time ; and if it be only ten pounds a year more, you will be glad of it when you are old."

Renie did not tell that she had already tried.

" You are going to stay some time, are you not, Miss Trufit ?"

" Well, till after Christmas, I trust ; that is, if *I* don't clash with Lady Rudkin. I must ask you to keep your eye on me, Renie, and cry out when I am getting warm, as the children do."

CHAPTER XIII.

THE arrival of the little old lady gave a new
colouring to things. She quite unintentionally
sat down in precisely the piace Sir Bevis had
mentioned to Renie as wishing her to occupy,
and talked and chatted to the young people
in a strain so droll and lively, that she quite
won the hearts of Rufus, Lucy, and Renie.
Sir Bevis looked and listened with a happier
face than Renie had seen him wear for a
month, and she resolved that Miss Priscilla
should remain, since she promised to fill the
place so well. She had not been in the house

many days before she asked Renie with her knitting needles poised gracefully in the air—

" Where did your uncle pick up that polished scamp ?"

" Who ! exclaimed Renie sharply. " Mr. Sebastain ?"

" Dear me, no, Renie ; how could you think I meant him. I allude to that Mr. Gunstan."

The circumstance was duly explained to Miss Trufit, also his position with respect to the estate, and at the conclusion she rocked her white head from side to side. Lucy Northwood kicked Renie triumphantly, and they both waited to hear the old lady's opinion ; but they were disappointed, she said nothing.

Just about this time Mr. Twinkleton wrote to Renie, and remitted a good round sum for the last pictures. She had now certain employment ; as fast as she could paint them he could sell, and he also, like a kind-hearted old man, named her to a dealer who wished to sell for her. So that Renie might truly say she was rising in spite of difficulties.

The cutting wind gave nearly everyone cold, and among the rest was strong Renie. Miss Priscilla, who had taken a great liking to the dear girl, made her a hot potion, and gave Lucy strict orders on no account to let her throw the bed clothes off. All this Lucy faithfully promised to do; but I am afraid Renie was not a good patient, for when bedtime arrived she made Christie leave a big box of coal, and coolly sitting down in front of the blaze, announced her intention of writing letters.

"I am not really ill, Lucy, and feel wide awake, so I will just post up my correspondence, which is frightfully in arrears."

"Yes, and in the morning you will be very ill, and Miss Trufit will dance mad. Leave your letters alone, Renie, you will make yourself out and out ill, and then you will be satisfied."

" Not I ; and listen, there is a copy of
' Wuthering Heights' on that shelf, just you
read it ; you won't want to go to bed when
you get transplanted to 'Thrushcross
Grange.' "

Either Lucy was weak and could not resist
the treat of reading a good novel, or Renie
was decidedly strong, for it ended in Renie's
jug of hot mixture being put by the fire and
the two girls making themselves comfortable.
They both became deaf to all sounds, had
any penetrated to the west wing, and there is
no telling how long they would have sat had
not Renie moved her position, and her flannel
sleeve catching a calendar box, knocked it
down. Lucy looked up.

" What are you about ?"

" Clumsiness as usual, Miss Northwood.
But just look at the clock, Lucy ?"

Lucy did ; the hands said a quarter past
one.

" Well, we've done it this time, and I am

cold now I come to myself.   How's the gruel?
Cold, my love; cold as tea, except the top of
the plate, and that's nearly baked. Everyone's
in bed and asleep ages ago, only we might as
well be screwed in our coffins as in this west
wing, no sound rambles down *here* with the
doors shut.   What's to be done?"

"Miss Priscilla will whip me in the morning when she hears how we obeyed her orders.
We should both be the better for something
hot. Stay, I know what I'll do. I'll step
down to Mrs. Troost's parlour and see if there
is anything in that closet, and get her pretty
little kettle.   We can easily boil some water
and warm the cockles of our hearts."

Renie made no objection, beyond warning
her not to be frightened when she got there
and drop the things with a shout.

"No fears," as baby would say. "Give
me that night-light, and I'll be there and
back before you've written 'Yours ever,
Renie.'"

Lucy was ready and off, her legs taking strides large enough for a giant. The corridors were awfully quiet and gloomy, and the paintings that by day looked so bewitching now appeared hideous as Lucy glided past them. She was cautious and light of foot, and reached the bottom of the stairs in safety, but there she paused, and her eyes gradually dilated. The house was in pieces, and had as many passages and sharp corners as if it had been an underground habitation. It was towards one of these dark openings that Lucy was looking. Her quick eyes detected a faint glimmer of light on the polished floor. At the end of that inlet there was only one room, and that Sir Bevis's study. Could he be up so late? No, surely not; he had all the day to write and read. Curiosity is strong in woman, it is their gift from Mother Eve; she tempted Adam to eat the forbidden fruit, and the consequence was their eyes were opened. This was precisely what Lucy desired to do to hers; she wanted to see who was in that room. There was only one way, and that was to look in. So, catching up her skirt she stepped down the passage. The door was closed all but a little space, through which the light streamed, but Lucy could see nothing because it did not face the centre of the apartment—it was at one end, and there was no gap by the hinges, the wood was too thick and the door fitted too well. Push it Lucy dared not. So there was nothing for it but to listen. Suddenly there was a rustle of dry paper, and a hurried, low exclamation.

"Deuce take it; might as well hunt for a needle in a hay stack. That little fool's told me a lie, d— her."

The speaker moved, and a chair sounded on the carpet.

He was coming out; there was no time to fly. Lucy put out the night-light with her hand and drew herself up behind the door. She was not a second too soon; the mysterious visitor came out, but so abrupt was he in his movements, that, instead of shading his candle with his hand, he held it high up, and the strong current of cold air whistling down the passage and meeting it, put it out. He came to a dead stop for a second, and then commenced swearing so horribly under his breath that Lucy felt ready to scream from terror. They were now both in the dark, and he was groping along the walls, muttering oaths at every step. Once he was so close to Lucy that she felt his hot breath upon her cheek. He had lost himself quite, and kept saying—

"If once I could get out of this cursed passage I could manage."

The scraping as he felt his way along at last grew fainter, and Lucy guessed he had gone. She, therefore, crept out of the corner and began her journey back to the west wing, for, of course, she could not go to Mrs. Troost's parlour in the dark. She could hear her heart thumping as she crept along the corridor and, getting into the room, dropped into a chair.

" Lucy, for heaven's sake what's the matter ?" cried Renie, jumping up, " are you ill ?"

" No, no, dear, I shall be all right directly. I have had an adventure, Renie, an encounter, in short, an awful fright. I never reached Mrs. Troost's room, and you look so pale, dear ?"

" And so do you, Lucy ; here, come to the fire, and I will go down this time !"

" Well, it is all safe now, Renie, but I had much rather you stayed here ; I am all right, and perhaps we could contrive to warm that stuff ?"

" Yes, if it were wanted, but it is not ; I am not ill, you have put my cold to flight. I am burning to hear your adventure !"

Lucy did not keep Renie waiting long ; she related her strange encounter precisely as it occurred, which is a thing very few can manage to do. At the close there was none of the burning perceptible in Renie's face that she had mentioned as feeling at the beginning. She was perfectly colourless. Neither of the girls spoke, and the echo of Lucy's voice seemed long in departing.

"Renie, are you dumb, or considering the politest mode of telling me I have imagined it?"

"Neither, Lucy; I am struggling with terror, with a nameless dread that creeps over me on all sides," and the girl shivered and drew closer to the fire.

Presently she spake again.

"You did not see his face, Lucy? You have no idea who he was?"

"No, I did not see his face, nor any part of him, the candle going out prevented that, and the darkness was dense. But I can *guess*, you know, Renie."

"Yes, I know you can—who was it, Lucy?"

"Leopold Gunstan, as you already suspect."

"Yes, but what could he be doing there?"

"Reading, my dear. Papers sometimes bear strange interest, especially where there is a question of title and estate."

"Ah, Lucy, surely—"

"Surely nothing, Renie. Let us leave it alone, I cannot prove it, as you told me about the window affair, so I prefer letting it be. I only wish something could be advised to get rid of the fellow. He makes no sign of moving!"

"Not one; he is too comfortable to do that, but he has not prolonged his visit beyond the rules of politeness, for all that. He has not been here quite three weeks, and I heard uncle, on the second or third day, ask him to remain the month out."

"Indeed! then I wish the month were out; but it is 'an ill wind that blows nobody any good,' and perhaps this may blow your cold away!"

"It has already; I feel no symptom of it, beyond a pain in my head."

In the morning Miss Priscilla pronounced Renie feverish, and questioned Lucy about how she had fulfilled her instructions, in answer to which she replied that she had done so to the best of her ability. What that best was, Miss Trufit did not inquire.

Addy was more at Zeiglehcath than ever just now, for Miss Priscilla doated on her, and fondled and made such fuss over Mrs. Howard that Norman declared he should get jealous. But the little old lady was not daunted, and Addy liked nothing half so well as to carry Miss Trufit off with her now and then. Pretty little Mrs. Addy never seemed quite at her ease in the presence of Lady Rudkin, and it rather amused Renie. But Miss Trufit agreed with her that my lady was now frequently out of temper, and the two took their complaints to Renie one day, when she had a pain in her head, and was sitting over the

H 5

fire. The cold was a long time going, and often the brown face was flushed. Miss Priscilla called it " condensed cold," and Renie let her have it her own way. It was safer than entering into an explanation.

" Renie, *do* come and stay with us, dear," said Addy.

" No, thank you, Addy, not at present ;" and she turned wearily to the fire.

" Norman made me promise to bring you back, and I asked uncle about it."

" And what did he say to it ?"

" Well, he seemed rather disappointed, I thought. I am afraid he is getting selfish. You have not been over to us for a week."

" What a long time," replied Renie, smiling. " You can have Lucy, if you like, but why don't you and Norman come here oftener, Addy."

" Ah ! I don't know, I think it is because Lady Rudkin is cross."

" Cross ?"

"Well, out of temper slightly, don't you agree with me, Miss Priscilla?"

"Yes. I must say I do, my dear. Your sister is right, Renie. Lady Rudkin has been peevish the last week or so; you don't perceive it, because you are not much with her; but everything appears a trouble to her, and she is so dreadfully fidgety, she scarcely sits still three minutes together."

"By the way, Renie, Norman met the Count the other day at the saddler's, and they walked home together; he asked after the ladies most politely."

"Indeed. I like your Count, Addy."

A few more commonplace remarks, and the startling news that the Curate's wife, poor young creature, had been confined with twins that morning at a quarter-past six, and Mrs. Addy settled her hat, shook out her flounces, and took her departure, to be greeted by her best of husbands with an affectionate kiss and a fervent "God bless you," as if she had been absent four months instead of four hours. But things were at Beach Cliff as they ought to be in every house, which, alas, they are *not*. Too many wives are literally terrified of their husbands, and look at them each day as they return from business to see if they are in a " good temper." To live in a house where such is the case, produces an impression never to be forgotten, and it is worse still to see and hear brothers swearing and fighting, pulling handfulls of hair out of each other's heads, and, by way of change, the father fighting with the sons. A house which is a polite sort of menagerie, where superiority is only maintained by brute force. To see sons rant and swear at their mother and sisters, fling down chairs and shake the very room with their temper ; to see that mother, poor weak woman, frightened—and not without cause—of those sons who ought to be a stay and a comfort to her shortening days is not calculated to impress one with a favour-

able opinion of wedded life. And these are
men that women are supposed to look up to
and rely upon? God forbid; and yet, they
are created after the image of Our Lord, who
would not have set His foot upon a worm.
For such a family there can be but one wish
—may the race become extinct. May there
be no males, and may the females, grafted into
a pure stock, where Truth reigns supreme,
produce children with better principles, more
manliness, and less brutality. Many a life is
saddened and embittered by harsh words and
unkindness, and when that life is a mother's,
surely the reward for the children is ever-
lasting damnation, and a just one.

CHAPTER XIV.

.

THE dining-room presented a well-to-do, cheerful appearance this cold evening, as the family sat at dinner. But the master was rather silent and depressed.

" Uncle," said Renie softly, " are you not well ?"

" Yes, thank you, my dear, quite well. That is, as well as usual. I think you ought to try some mutton in place of that dry chicken, Renie."

" Oh no, I like this better."

" But meat is more strengthening. Pro-

mise me to try and keep well, to take care of
yourself."

The tone, though low, was eager, and
Renie, in astonishment, hastened to reply—

" Yes, I promise, uncle, but it is unneeded,
I am in good health."

" Which wine, sir ?" asked the butler.
Three times had the man spoken, and still no
answer.

" Uncle, which will you take, Moselle or
Hock ?" said Renie, bending to him.

" Eh ? what wine ? Neither, my dear,
neither." And he slipped off into his dream
again.

The weather prevented any rambles, at
least for the ladies, so that the drawing-room
was resorted to immediately after dinner.
When the gentlemen came in Sir Bevis did
not follow, and Renie, after watching some
time, betook herself to the piano. Presently
Miss Trufit exclaimed—

" I wonder what has become of them all ?"

Renie stopped playing and looked round. There were only Miss Priscilla, Lucy, and Rufus Sebastain, buried in a volume of Tennyson, on a remote couch.

"Oh," spake Lucy, looking up from her work, "Sir Bevis has never been in, and Lady Rudkin only remained a short time. Mr. Gunstan has been gone precisely twenty minutes by the clock."

"What an invaluable witness you would make, Miss Northwood; such decided evidence as that would convict anyone. Time is the most difficult point in a trial; it is rarely that a witness is sure to five or ten minutes."

"Well, Mr. Sebastain, I cannot take all the credit —"

There was a muffled sound at the door, and Lady Rudkin walked in, with a face as hard as steel, followed by Leopold Gunstan.

"My dear Lady Rudkin, has anything happened?" asked Miss Trufit, advancing towards her.

The face may be easily controlled, not so the voice. As long as my lady kept her mouth shut all well and good, but the instant she attempted to answer Miss Priscilla, that organ showed itself master, and rose in a discordant little shriek.

" Now, my dear Lady Rudkin," said Leopold Gunstan, " let me entreat you to be calm ; compose yourself."

" I am composed, I assure you, Mr. Gunstan, only I—I—"

" Dear, dear, poor thing, a great shock ; but be calm, I beg, my dear madam."

My lady was not composed, no more were the others. " Tennyson" was on its back on the floor ; the only composed one was Mr. Gunstan.

" What is the matter ?" asked Renic, eyeing first one and then the other.

" Why, it is a most awful thing, and I don't want to shock you more than I can help," replied the composed wanderer. " The fact is your uncle has been seized with a fit in his study, and he has—died in that fit, Miss Renie."

Miss Priscilla set up a dismal wail, and the artist, shocked out of all propriety, exclaimed—

" Good God !"

" Yes, it is so indeed. Lady Rudkin, pray sit down. Nay, Miss Rudkin, let me entreat you not to go, I have sent for a doctor, and it is better not to alarm the house."

He stood barring the way to the door, but now his face seemed just a shade altered in colour. Rufus Sebastain was close to Renie, and they were all white and silent. It was an unnatural, constrained silence, the news seemed to have paralysed everyone. The only person who had raised her voice in lamentation was Miss Trufit, and she now sat rocking her small body to and fro in agony. Lady Rudkin had sat down as requested, and steeled her beautiful face again.

There was no trace of tears, her eyes were hard and dry, and bent on the carpet. The one solitary sign of emotion was displayed in her hands. The fingers writhed and twisted perpetually, like worms.

Leopold Gunstan was smiling in a would-be sympathetic but decidedly sickly fashion, and Renie was looking at him rather contemptuously.

"Mr. Gunstan, Sir Bevis is my uncle; he is nothing to you; allow me to pass?"

The man at once obeyed, and moved as if to accompany her.

"No, stay where you are, I can find my way. Mr. Sebastain, do you come with me?"

"Certainly, Miss Rudkin, if you wish it."

The study door was reached, and found to be locked when Rufus gently tried it. Mrs. Troost and Frost now joined them, for the news had spread in spite of Mr. Gunstan's precaution. The old butler was not so composed as the wanderer could have wished, when he dispatched the message.

"It is locked, Miss Rudkin. What is to be done?"

"Go round by my lady's morning-room," sobbed the housekeeper.

That was found accessible, and they passed in, and opened the door of communication. Both rooms had lamps burning in them, and in the study a bright fire. The flame blazed up every now and then, and near to it, with his face turned towards the window, sat the baronet. The countenance was not distorted, and the proud mouth looked as if smiling. He had died smiling; smiling with happiness. Renie glanced at the window; the shutters were not closed, and the snow was falling silently in great white flakes. She remembered how years ago his love had died on just such a night; no wonder he smiled.

"Ah, dear me!" moaned old Frost, "to think my poor old master should have died like this, setting here in his chair."

"It must have been a quiet fit, for he looks as if he slept, and his eyes are shut," remarked Mrs. Troost.

Renie and Rufus said nothing, and shortly after they left the room.

At the door stood Lucy.

"Well, is it true?"

"True!" echoed Rufus Sebastain, in astonishment; "it is too true, Miss Northwood."

"Yes, yes, I know that; but the fit—is that true?"

Renie's tongue clove to the roof of her mouth, and again Rufus spoke.

"Yes; he must have died in some sort of fit. I have lost a kind, kind friend. Do you want to go in, Miss Lucy?"

"No, thank you; there is someone there, is there not?"

" Yes. Frost and Mrs. Troost."

A draught of cold air announced the approach of the doctor. He came forward with a face a suitable length for the occasion, and a professional bend of the back. They had got the nearest, the one lately set up in the village, Doctor Sibbley Bacup. He was not supposed to be depending upon his practice, but that was, of course, a matter of opinion.

His appearance was rather pleasing ; not a decidedly handsome man, and yet able to pass for such. His face was dark and ruddy ; his body stout, as is generally the case with country people ; his age possibly forty-eight. This was his first visit to Zeigleheath, but Renie knew him by sight, though he did not know who she was, so made a guess.

" Lady Rudkin, I believe ?"

" No, I am not Lady Rudkin. Mrs. Troost, will you show the way ?"

" Allow me to save you the trouble, Mrs. Troost ; I will undertake that office."

The speaker was Leopold Gunstan, and without giving time for a refusal he led the way, followed by the elated doctor.

At such times as the present it is a difficult task to unite events ; a household visited by death is always for a period disjointed, and when all is quiet and the links are coupled, it is amazing what a length the chain is, and how much has escaped notice. The others went back to the drawing-room.

Lady Rudkin was sitting just as they had left her, and Miss Trufit was like a wise Christian, doing her best to make her cry, and immediately informed Renie, in a loud whisper, that the poor thing would never be relieved till she died.

But my lady obstinately refused to be relieved, in default of which Miss Priscilla wept enough for both.

After a lapse of five or ten minutes Mr. Gunstan appeared, and, in a subdued tone, told them that Dr. Bacup pronounced death to have been caused by paralysis of the heart, and they were going to take the body up-stairs.

No one objected ; and Mr. Gunstan, having taken everything on his own shoulders as the nearest male relative present, departed to see this order executed. It was done as quietly as possible ; Leopold Gunstan took the head and Doctor Bacup the feet, Frost watching the process, and in that manner the remains of the old man were carried up to his room.

Then followed a silence, and then a solemn stir, as the last master for many years to come was taken with becoming state and pomp to his final resting place. The next baronet was that golden-headed baby boy up-stairs, with his soft nose flat against the glass, watching " poor papa " from nurse's knee. It was a fine place to go masterless so long, and a great place to hold in trust.

Norman and Addy were dreadfully cut up at the sudden death of the old gentleman, but Norman's sorrow melted before his surprise when Renie told him of her trust.

"My dear girl, it is no small undertaking. Whatever induced your uncle to saddle you with such a responsibility?"

"I don't know, Norman. I could not refuse; he seemed to wish it so much. At any price I am prepared to carry out his orders, and do my duty as far as I am able."

"Yes, I feel sure you are, Renie; but—" and Norman finished the sentence by a dubious shake of his head.

Mrs. Addy, like a wise little woman, burst into tears when she was told, and declared there would never be an end to the trouble. They both took a decidedly gloomy view of the case, and Renie opened her eyes.

"Well, what is wrong with you two? It is too late to retract now, even if I felt disposed, which I don't. Uncle trusted me, and his trust shall not be misplaced by any fault or neglect of mine. I will do the best I can,

and take care of the child and his money.
But, Norman, you must second my sugges-
tions if I make any, for Lady Rudkin knows
nothing of this arrangement."

"You may be sure I will, but it will give
her a pill; it is the queerest thing I ever
heard of. Your uncle must have had some
strong motive for giving all power to you."

"Perhaps; for he seemed determined I
should accept the post."

Norman was correct; it was a pill, and not
alone for my lady, but for all others, and
they regarded Renie, sitting there so modestly,
in wonderment.

When Mr. Chalmers had explained the will
to them, and pointed to Renie as the mistress
of all till the boy should attain his majority,
Lady Rudkin gave a faint gasp—

"Then I am cut off?"

"No, Lady Rudkin; your late husband
insured his life, and paid an enormously heavy
premium which brings you in two hundred a
year."

" And that is *all* ?"

" Yes, all."

My lady wiped her lip; there was blood
upon it; the pearly teeth were long and
sharp.

" And is there no mention of anyone else ?"
asked her ladyship.

" Yes, there are a few legacies to old
servants, and the ' sum of a hundred a year
for my beloved niece, Renie Dorothy, as long
as she shall live.' That is private, and has
nothing to do with the income from the pro-
perty, which Miss Rudkin can spend in main-
taining this establishment while she is the
little heir's guardian, if she deems proper.
Everything is in her hands."

The intelligence was startling, but, the
panic over, things began to steady themselves.
There was one class in the house who hailed
the new government with joy and thankful-
ness, and that was the staff of old retainers.
They all cried with one accord that their late

master had done well in making Miss Renie mistress.

How did the young mistress bear her honours? With a calm, self-possessed dignity; there was no ruffling, she gradually gathered all the reins into her steady hand and held them with a light, but firm grasp. She did not check them, and she knew when and where to give headway. Her manner towards Lady Rudkin was thoughtful and courteous, but that lady did not appear quite conscious of external things; she was always pre-occupied.

Rufus Sebastain made ready for departure, but Renie coolly inquired—

" Are the paintings done ?"

" No, Miss Rudkin, not quite; but I will take them with me, and forward them when completed."

" It is scarcely worth while, Mr. Sebastain. I had rather you stayed till they are finished. Lucy, dear, the butter ?"

The matter was thus arranged before the breakfast partakers with perfect ease; and Leopold Gunstan fidgetted. He perceived that his turn was to come, and he was not out in his reckoning. *He* had no pictures to finish, but he had made no sign of leaving, for which Renie had patiently waited.

Evidently he presumed, from his round-about connection with the family, but that was not going to be permitted. So, watching a suitable opportunity when there was no one present, she said—

" Mr. Gunstan, has it never occurred to you to go ?"

He started visibly, and made answer—

" Sir Bevis asked me to stay."

" I am aware of that, and the given time has not *quite* expired. But let me remind you that when death takes place all previous arrangements are null. In short—I wish you to go ; and the sooner you set about it the better I shall be pleased."

He smiled, and in a tone that meant to imply deeply wounded feelings, replied—

" I am sorry you should still continue to regard me as a stranger. You have been most persistent in doing that, Miss Rudkin, ever since I came, but I did hope that at such a time as the present you would have relented, and remembered the relationship."

She turned upon him sharply.

" Your hopes are useless, Mr. Gunstan, since I happen to know what that relationship really is. You are nothing to me or my family; and I look upon you as an interloper. If by staying here you imagine your claim will be recognised, you are mistaken, so you may as well give up sheltering yourself under the wing of relationship, connection, or anything else. This is your first visit, but it is your last while I reign here."

He gazed in astonishment at the decided girl who so resolutely faced him. He could not flatter, and he could not frighten her.

The arched eyebrows raised themselves in-differently, he displayed his white fangs bewitchingly, and set about beating as amiable and brave a retreat as possible.

" You possess a quality not frequently to be found in the softer sex; you speak to the purpose, Miss Rudkin, and that is what few do. There is no possibility of misunder-standing you."

" I don't intend that you should misunder-stand me, Mr. Gunstan. There is a 'time table' in the library, and no doubt you will be able to find a train to suit you, or a drag can take you to a neighbouring village."

She did not wait for his reply, but, wishing him good-bye, left the room. The door shut, and Leopold Gunstan made one or two short runs up and down the room like a caged tiger, and then coming to a stand with his back to the fire, drew his coat tails under his arms. Perhaps the warmth was soothing, for he half smiled, and said—

" Plenty of pluck, and no buttering toler-
ated *there*.　It's a case of ' take care of yourself, Mr. Gunstan ;'　the presiding angel is
not a woman, but a head."

Meanwhile the " head " journied on till she
met Lady Rudkin. Her ladyship did not wear
a widow's cap, and her beautiful hair was
gathered up carelessly. Her heavy black dress
was relieved by cuffs and collar of white, not
unlike those used by the " Sisters of Mercy."
Renie thought how sweet she looked, for her
face was thin, and the eyes glittering as if
from fever.

" Renie," asked the young widow, " what
are the rooms being changed for ?"

There was a twinge of irritation in the
tone.

" Because I ordered it, Lady Rudkin.　I
intend to make several alterations, one of the
first being the departure of Mr. Gunstan."

My lady's lips moved, but no sound came,
and Renie passed on.

It was hard to determine which feeling it
was that agitated the girlish figure standing
there, disappointment or relief; but there was
certainly more elasticity as she hurried on towards the great hall. There she hesitated as
if uncertain how to proceed; but making a
dash at the library door, opened it and entered.
The room was not empty. Mr. Gunstan had
followed Renie's directions without much
delay, and was now bending over the "time
table."

"Ah! my dear Lady Rudkin, just in time
to say adieu to me."

"Then you *are* going?"

"Yes, I am; ar'n't you relieved? Never
mind, the best of friends must part, eh?"

"I suppose so, but I did not think it was
at once."

"Did you not? Miss Rudkin is a most
decided lady, and takes everything by the
horns, instanter. I hope she won't take you
by *yours*, Esther, my dear; you have been

living on clover here; and the munificent sum
of two hundred pounds per annum would only
purchase hay in the present state of the
market."

"But *must* you go, Leopold?"

"Yes, I am told to pick a train or take a
drag; but I am to *go*, and what is more, not
come again. There is no treating with Miss
Rudkin, my dear, so don't you attempt it.
But ' parting is such sweet sorrow,' that I can
say good-bye until—when?"

"No, no, Leopold," cried my lady, snatch-
ing away her hand; "*no!*"

He laughed the old satanic laugh.

"Well, we will not say adieu; but *au
revoir*."

My lady said nothing, and he left.

Miss Northwood was standing at the nursery
window with Rodney in her arms as the drag
wheeled through the trees.

"Why, there's Mr. Gunstan, luggage and
all; is he going?"

"Yes," replied Renie, glancing up from a drawing of pigs and cows for her charge, "he is going, and—for good."

"The Lord be praised!" fervently ejaculated nurse.

Both the girls started.

"You are not prepossessed with Mr. Gunstan, Mary?"

"No, Miss Renie, I am not. I'd as lief be prepossessed with the devil. I would," and she set down the iron with a bang.

There were several things to be arranged, and the one first taken in hand was securing the services of Miss Priscilla Trufit. That lady had, like Rufus Sebastain, prepared to leave, but Renie kindly offered her a home at Zeigleheath. Words could not express the old lady's delight and gratitude, so she clasped the amazed Renie in her arms.

"Yes, my dear, I will stay, and gladly, as long as you choose. I am happy with you."

"I am very glad to hear it, Miss Trufit,

and I shall ask Lucy to remain on a long visit, there will be just an even number then. I must always have someone, for I dare not be left too long alone with Lady Rudkin."

"No. I fancy she has changed, Renie, since the death of poor cousin Bevis; she is so nervous and thin, in fact, queer."

That was the most appropriate term; Lady Rudkin *was* queer, Miss Priscilla had hit it. Lucy said she reminded her of a person walking in her sleep, and Miss Lucy was not far wrong. She sat from morning till night without doing anything. When she walked it was as Lucy said. She rarely, if ever, exerted herself to talk, and always seemed thinking deeply. Till at last she slipped out of their intercourse, beyond the usual rules of politeness and her presence. Miss Trufit said it was the reaction after the sudden shock, and that a decided change would be beneficial. Renie immediately proposed that

she and Mrs. Shepperton should go away, but
this my lady stoutly refused to do.

The establishment was reduced by Renie's
order to half its size, some of the servants were dismissed, and only a sufficient
number kept. Several of the horses and
carriages were sold, the staff of men reduced
to three, and the rooms not required closed
up. Renie was not going to keep a place for
servants; the heir was a child, and could not
take pleasure in such grandeur, so the money
should be put aside for him to devote to a
wiser purpose when he could have a voice
in the matter.

Norman Howard thought Renie very wise,
but Lady Rudkin appeared dissatisfied. She
was Lady Rudkin without a say in anything;
she was divested of all power to act. It was
not an enviable position, certainly, but then
it was not Renie's fault. Indeed, it was just
a question who had the most disagreeable
place of it, the aunt or the niece.

CHAPTER XV.

THE winter sun is setting over the cliffs, and the sea song comes with the breeze, and blends mournfully with the rustling leaves in a long sob of pain. The wind is inquisitive, and searches the face of yonder maiden; it cannot be well paid for its pains, for it rushes off again, with a shrill whistle, into the almost naked woods. And yet that maiden is its foster child; she is wild, like the wind, and they have sported and run races together many a day. But now Princess Althea is sad, and tears are streaming from the beautiful eyes.

Her cheeks are sunken, and her step no longer buoyant—her feet drag. Is she reluctant to quit the ground?

'Yes; the King has given the word to march, and a sound of hammering is already audible. The gipsy girl has not had a meeting with her noble love for long; the weather was too cold, in spite of her prayers to the Virgin for heat. She watches from every part, but he does not come, and why? Because he has already gone, and her image does not trouble his bad heart.

"And I wanted to ask him if— No, no; he *is* my love, and he'll be sorry when he finds I'm gone. Leopold, dearest, good-bye."

She raised herself on her small feet, and, with eyes strained in the direction of Zeigle-heath, kissed her hand. The action was so pretty, so artless, the glowing face yet wet with tears so reflected the soul's light of which the wanderer was the centre, that it was a pity earthly eyes could not witness it, as well as heavenly ones. When the watery moon was sitting on her high throne, lending a feeble light, a team of waggons, accompanied by tall, noiseless figures, moved along the river's bank, with the hounds by their side. They made no sound, they bade no farewells ; those birds of passage had no leave-takings, and all they left to mark their stay were a few heaps of ashes.

There was one point in which Renie strictly obeyed her uncle, and that was in having little Rodney with her as much as possible. The nurseries were moved nearer to the west wing, and larger rooms selected. The studio was the scene of many a game of play, and Rufus Sebastain, instead of objecting, assisted at them. There was not many more days' work at the pictures, and Rufus sighed as he said it.

" You are sorry to go, Mr. Sebastain ?"

" Very, Miss Northwood; this is the only taste of home I have ever had, and I am loth to part from it."

" Well, the parting need not be a long one," said Renie, mindful of her uncle's words—'Don't lose sight of Rufus Sebastain.' " I shall always be pleased to see you."

" Many thanks; but would Lady Rudkin feel the same, do you think ?"

" Of course, and whether or no, it would make no difference, beyond perhaps being more agreeable for you. Miss Trufit and I will *always* give you a welcome, Mr. Sebastain."

" That is kind of you, Miss Rudkin. I may write to you sometimes ?"

" Yes, every week, if you choose," replied Renie, laughing. " There ! I have daubed my sleeve !"

One day Renie, passing through the hall, remembered that she had left a note for the early post on the library table, and told no one to take it. So she went to get it, and opening the door very suddenly, was in time to hear Lady Rudkin say—

"Indeed, you must be patient; it is not in my power at present."

The person she addressed was Doctor Bacup. Renie stopped with the door in her hand. The Doctor bowed, and said—

"Ah! You are anxious to hear my report of your *dear* aunt, Miss Rudkin? Very natural, I am sure; and, doubtless, to you, in suspense, our interview has been long. However, I am happy to be able to relieve your anxiety—"

"You mistake, sir. I am in no anxiety, nor had I any notion that Lady Rudkin required medical advice. My errand here is to get a letter I left, and now I have it."

The amiable practitioner smiled.

"Lady Rudkin is a trifle upset with the severe ordeal she has so lately passed through, in being deprived of the tender and watchful care of our lamented and esteemed—nay, I may say, beloved friend—"

There is no telling where his warmth of feeling would have carried him, had not Renie's face put his tender emotion to flight. Miss Rudkin was regarding him with curled lips and eyes rippling with fun, while she looked him over composedly.

"Astonishing! You are quite a genius, Doctor Bacup, and I fear you will never get properly appreciated in Moordart. Had I been aware of your ability, I might possibly have got you to write my uncle's biography. You could not have failed to do it justice, considering that you know nothing of his life or him, never even exchanged a word with him, and that your residence in this place can be compassed by months only, and those numbered on one hand. Lady Rudkin, since you are out of health, why did you not consult Mr. Owen, who was here no later than tyeserday? *He* has attended here for years."

"I really don't know, Renie; I seemed to shrink from the recollection of past days," and her ladyship put up her handkerchief.

Doctor Bacup came to the rescue.

"To be sure, to be sure; Miss Rudkin must kindly make allowances for whims and over-wrought nerves. But I hope" (with a bland smile) "to be able to set your dear aunt to rights in a few days."

With a freezing bow Renie left the room. She could not order the man out simply because she disliked him, and especially when Lady Rudkin had sent for him; surely he would see he was not wanted.

Lucy was astonished when Renie told her of her interview.

"It is certainly a queer way to speak to one's doctor. 'Indeed you must be patient; it is not in my power at present.' I don't see what such a speech could have have to do with ailments, do you?"

"Not clearly, and yet it must."

" Perhaps he was suggesting that she should rouse herself, and a very good thing if she did too."

Lucy smiled.

"Your aunt won't expire of grief, Renie, though she carries such a dejected, contrite face. The pretty girlish creature is harder inside than out. Why did you not give the man to understand (as you are so well able to do) that his room was more to be desired than his company."

" I did plainly."

" Then depend upon it he won't come again."

But Miss Northwood was wrong. He did come, and always contrived to spin out the time pretty well. My lady still looked sad, and talked no more, though she took his medicine. Perhaps she had no faith; certainly Miss Rudkin had none.

The time came for Rufus Sebastain to leave. It was a fine Tuesday, and the very wind was gentle that day; it was one of those kind freaks of Mother Nature's that enables us to sport abit in the sunshine during the bleak dreary season. The shore was alive with the fishermen's children, dancing before the sunbeams and dipping their naked feet into the good-tempered sea; others sat mending nets by the rocks or under the shelter of an upturned boat. They had no fears, those Neptune's babies, and crawled along the slabs of narrow slippery rock, where it seemed impossible for mortal to stand, seeking birds' nests in summer. They were safe on the beach, every mother appeared to consider the ocean a nurse.

Rufus Sebastain was standing at the window looking over the sea. Presently he called—

" Miss Rudkin, come here ? See," and he pointed, " the tide is going out, and when I came it was coming in. Is it not queer ? does it know I am leaving. I am inclined to think it is symbolical of my life, and that I

am going out with the tide. It leaves no
trace, no footsteps to mark its visit; no more
shall I."

"Nonsense; you are moody, Mr. Sebastain."

And Renie looked at him just a shade
anxiously.

It was not a thing to do under ordinary
circumstances, for this friendless artist was
nothing to her. Nothing? Yes, he was
something to her, a great something; he was
the being she loved best on earth. Renie had
not found out all at once that she loved Rufus
Sebastain, and when she did make the startling discovery, the blood rushed into her
cheeks, and she took good care to keep the
knowledge to herself. Was it anything to be
ashamed of? No. But she was rather awk-
wardly placed.

Lucy Northwood was correct, Platonic
friendship *was* a dangerous game to play at,
only Lucy's fears had been for the wrong

person. The artist was, to all appearances,
safe, while Renie—the strong, fire-proof Renie
—had got netted. She had begun to befriend
him because she liked him, and saw a light
under a bushel, as the Count would have said.
She was frank by nature, and he had trusted
her as a brother might, and talked freely.
That was the ground they had started on, and
for anything Renie knew to the contrary he
was on it still; but she was not, her stand
was now a nearer and dearer one. How was
she to make him see it? If Cupid did not
shoot a dart before his eyes, she could not.
There was nothing but to be silent and wait.
She might well regard him anxiously, he was
depressed, and needed cheering; but where
was the kind, sisterly feeling, the strong, dis-
interested words?

Ah! me—it *was* a mistake!

" I may indeed feel faint-hearted after such
a restful time spent here. I shall have no one
to take any interest in me when I lose you;

no one to care whether I go to perdition soul
and body."

"But you have not lost me yet, Mr. Sebastain; when you do, it will be time enough for
you to go."

She said this quite firmly, and there was
nothing to tell the tale, so he turned brightly
(he was a very creature of impulse this artist,
one moment sad the other happy), and holding
out his hand, said—

"One could not long be dismal with you,
for you are always the same, and have no
doubts and fears. I only wish I could be as
steadfast as you, Miss Rudkin. My mind is
always in the same state as the children's
game of 'see-saw,' one end up the other end
down, never parallel. But the time goes on,
and I want to ask you a great favour. Will
you give me that face, that fancy face you
did? You remember me finding it?"

Yes, she remembered perfectly well; also
whose face it was, and she hesitated.

"Please don't refuse me, Miss Rudkin, I will never part with it, I promise you, and will return it, if you will do me another. I would copy it myself, only I cannot get the same expression; my fancy for that face is more misty than yours. I see it perfectly only in my dreams. The angel to whom I gave that face in the picture I told you about is not so good as yours."

"That, then, was why you were so agitated upon finding it?"

"Yes, I saw the original of my face in the trees. It is a wonderful thing that you should have drawn the same out of your head. You never saw the lady, Miss Rudkin?"

"No, never," replied Renie, with brows knitted; "and I will give it to you on two conditions. First, that you never show it to anyone; secondly, that you never part with it excepting back to me; and if you are very ill destroy it. Will you take it now, Mr. Sebastain?"

He looked amazed; her face was ashy pale.

"Yes, I will have it, Miss Rudkin, and promise to fulfil these conditions."

The girl mounted a chair, and unlocking a corner cupboard, took out the portrait of Clorinda Rudkin, and gave it to the artist.

The cuckoo clock struck twelve, and re-minded Rufus Sebastain that there was such a thing as being too late for a train.

"I must be off. Good-bye, Miss Rudkin, kind friend; I will write often, since you allow me, and will never forget you."

"Stay a second, Mr. Sebastain; promise me something, and then you may go."

There was a compression about the mouth that told how sincere were the following words—

"Promise me that if ever you are in trouble of any sort you will come or send to me, or, if you are ill, come, and Miss Trufit shall nurse you."

The young man's eyes filled.

"You are too good to me. But I promise gladly. The money for the work I have just done will keep me some time, and I mean to be careful and industrious."

He smiled, and left the room, and Renie stood where he had left her, quite unconscious that great tears were rolling down her white face. But there was no trace of them when Lucy and little Rodney came in; she was bewildered rather than anything else. What could cause her aunt's face to haunt the poor artist? They had never met, for she was dead before he was born. Renie's senses were rather in a whirl, things had gone so oddly of late, and she was trying to find a way out of the maze, and could not.

The entrance of the little lad and Lucy made a happy break in her thoughts, and she turned with a long-drawn sigh of relief, like one waking from a horrid dream, to the fresh young child clambering on to her lap. He was a fine healthy boy, and she watched him

anxiously for his father's sake; he had left
her Rodney, and the small body was like a
mine of gold which she must never have long
out of her sight. Thank Heaven! he was
well and happy, and loved her dearly. That
was her first care, to win his whole heart,
since he was her sole charge to be for many
and many a year. He still wore a black frock
for "poor papa," but it was well covered by
his pinafore, for Renie did not like children in
mourning. His little bare neck was in layers
of fat, and the string of coral beads quite
bedded in the soft warm flesh. He *was* a
pretty lad.

"There, darling, sit still a minute; you
will make my knees quite sore."

"Poor aunty! poor aunty!" and he stroked
her face with his sticky fat fingers, for it
must be told unto you that he and Miss Lucy
had just been paying Mrs. Troost a visit, and
the little one had been hugging a canister of
cakes most affectionately.

" Who has sticky fingers ?"

" Rodney," and he buried his golden head in her bosom.

" I daresay he has," laughed Lucy. " We have been paying calls this morning, Aunt Renie, and lastly saw Mr. Sebastain drive off. I really felt disposed to cry, and most probably should, had not that young nobleman bitten his tongue, and therewith set up a terrific howl, which quite banished my tender feelings."

" It hurt Rodney, aunty," said the baby, putting the injured member out to its fullest length, possibly with the hope that she would " kiss it well."

But Renie had not got so far as that yet, though there is no telling what she might not have done at a pinch.

" Rodney, my boy, I advise you to put your tongue in, else it might refuse to go back if you keep it out any longer," said Lucy.

" Cousin Lucy a very naughty girl," responded that young gentleman composedly.

It was odd how he persisted in confusing the relationships. He called Lucy cousin, who was nothing to him, and Renie, who was cousin, aunt. But she never offered to correct him now, remembering his father's words. Renie sat quite silent, curling his soft hair round her fingers and wondering how it would be when he grew a great fellow, too big to sit on her knee.

" Renie," said Lucy abruptly, " I am right down sorry Mr. Sebastain has gone."

" Are you," responded Renie, absently staring out of the window.

They both seemed disposed to be thoughtful, only Rodney insisted on talking, and at last Renie sent him off.

CHAPTER XVI.

THINGS glided on peacefully enough over Christmas ; there was of course no merry making. Renie invited Norman and Addy for Christmas Day, so that Lady Rudkin might not feel it so much. But my lady seemed almost past feeling anything, and good tempered Norman regarded her in perplexity.

"Is she always like that?" asked he of Lucy.

" Yes, she sits and says nothing, and notices

nothing, not even the child. And he now never goes to her."

" Humph! its uncommonly odd, Miss Lucy; and how does Renie get along?"

" Oh! dear Renie, she goes on in the right way determinedly, in spite of dark looks. But, oh! Mr. Howard, I would not hold Renie's position for a good deal."

" Nor I."

Lady Rudkin's semi-sleeping state lasted till one afternoon, and then she suddenly awoke. It was getting late and quite dusk as Renie came up the stairs to her own rooms. The house was silent, and she heard distinctly the sobbing of a little voice. It was not near the nursery, else she would have suspected Rodney; it was close to my lady's apartments. Nevertheless she stopped, and while there heard the sound of slaps, and a harsh voice exclaimed—

" I'll teach you to say that again."

Before Renie could move nurse came flying along.

"Where's Sir Rodney, ma'am?"

There was no reply given, for Renie at once divined that it was he she had heard crying. The brown cheeks turned a deep red, and her clenched hand dealt the door a stinging blow.

"Open this door, Lady Rudkin, at once; you have Rodney here?"

There was a second's pause, and then a voice could be heard, as it neared the door, saying—

"My precious child, and did it knock its sweet little back. There—there."

It was not Lady Rudkin who spoke, and it was not Lady Rudkin who opened the door with little Rodney in her arms, trembling violently. At sight of Renie he stretched out his pretty arms, and bursting again into sobs cried—

"Take me, aunty."

Aunty was only too glad, and hugged him to her thankfully. Shepperton (for it was she) immediately began a long rigmarole of how he had followed her into her mistress's room and there knocked himself.

But Renie at once stopped her with—

"Silence, woman, you lie; you beat him, for I heard the slaps; you have done what you will never do again. Get ready to leave Zeigleheath."

The gaunt woman straightened her waist.

"I am here as Lady Rudkin's maid, not yours."

"Precisely, and I am here as mistress of you all. Where is Lady Rudkin?"

"Downstairs."

"Then go and tell her what I said, and don't lose any time over it."

With that Renie walked off, followed by nurse, boiling with indignation.

"So it has come to this, Miss Renie," said she, dealing the nursery fire a vigorous poke,

as Renie sat down in the rocking chair with
the child in her arms. " They have began
their games early, that they have; I don't
know rightly what is to become of us. You
will have hard work, Miss Renie, ma'am."

" What's the matter?" asked Lucy, coming
up to them.

" We've just had a scene, Miss Northwood," said nurse, turning and regarding her
shrewdly. " You are not surprised, are
you?"

" No," coolly replied Lucy, " I am not;
we shall be worse before we're better."

" Aye, aye, Miss Lucy!"

No more could be said, because the rustle
of silk became audible, and presently Lady
Rudkin, followed by Miss Trufit and Shepperton, entered the room. The two ladies
were dressed for dinner; it was their habit to
do so early, and then sit at work before the
drawing-room fire. My lady wore handsome
mourning, and it became her well. There

were jets in her golden hair to-night that sparkled and glittered with every movement of her head. Her face was perfectly pale, and the blue eyes had lost all look of sleep; my lady was at last awake. Miss Priscilla appeared bewildered, and took up her station by Renie—good old lady! Shepperton was rather green, as if seriously disturbed by her passion, and her nostrils opened and shut like valves. It was a curious sight, the armies drawn up in battle array, and the future king being gently rocked by his guardian. The weapons were to be tongues, justly called "two-edged swords."

Had Renie been disposed to commence the attack, my lady gave her no time to, for, sweeping up in front of her she said—

"Is it correct that you have told Shepperton, my maid, to go?"

"Perfectly correct, I did tell her so, and I now repeat it before you. She must go; I will not permit this child to be whipped at her pleasure."

"You don't know that she did whip him; ask him."

"I shall do nothing of the kind, Lady Rudkin; I am not going to cross-examine him for the benefit of your maid. My word is sufficient."

"But I will *not* part with her."

"Then there is but one alternative, Lady Rudkin, and that is for you to accompany her."

A dead silence followed this quiet speech, broken only by the slight creak of the rocking-chair. My Lady Rudkin recoiled, and then let the storm burst forth, heedless of witnesses.

"And I am to be told to go by *you*, a poor dependent niece! I am to be under your control, and have no word in anything—not even in that child. Never was there such gross injustice since the sun first rose and set! My husband was *persuaded* to leave everything to you ; he would never have done it of his own free will, but I will try my power, and see whether you can tell me to go as if I were a stranger."

It was hard to sit and be accused of double dealing ; but Renie showed no anger beyond a flush of the face.

" Very well, Lady Rudkin, you are at liberty to try anything you choose. I don't want *you* to go, only your maid, and you decline to be separated from the woman who beats your child. It is strange, such affection. With respect to your late husband leaving me full power, I imagine the cause of it to be best known to yourself. It was no doing of mine, God knows ; but since I am placed in authority, I will use it, and your maid Shepperton must go. If you are so much attached that you cannot part, why, you must go too."

There was a flutter, as if Lady Rudkin had something to say, only the words would not come, and no one assisting her, she retired from the field with her body-guard—Shepperton.

The first to speak was Miss Trufit. She put up her eye-glass, and came from behind Renie.

" My dear girl, what *have* you done ?"

" Told her ladyship to go, Miss Priscilla, since she won't let her nurse go without her."

" It seems to me, Miss Renie," said nurse, " that it's the maid who won't go without her ladyship."

Miss Trufit turned.

" That's a strange speech, nurse."

" Yes, it is, Miss Priscilla, but it suits the things. When we *see* queer things we mostly *say* queer things. I have been here longer than you, ma'am, and not slept both day and night."

" What shall you do, Renie ?"

" Nothing, unless she declines to go, and then I shall have her put out. I don't, of course, mean now, but towards the end of the week. I *can* do it, Miss Priscilla, and that Lady Rudkin will find out if she makes any resistance."

The house, of course, presented a most dismal appearance for the next few days. My lady kept her own apartment, and saw no one but Shepperton. Norman Howard came over and Mr. Chalmers was sent for. Both gentlemen were very sorry for the breach, but there was no way of mending it. Renie was unquestionably mistress, and a most determined one.

" I should like you to see Lady Rudkin, Mr. Chalmers, and hear what she has decided upon doing; whether she is willing to part with her maid."

The lawyer had an interview with her ladyship, and returned with the intelligence that sooner than separate from Shepperton she would go too.

" Then that ends it. You, of course, pay her her income, Mr. Chalmers, wherever she goes to."

" Certainly, Miss Rudkin. I cannot help saying I regret this quarrel."

" So do I. Not because I bear Lady Rudkin any affection, for I don't, but I wished to keep all peaceful round my uncle's memory. But could I allow that woman to beat Rodney without any cause but that he would not tell a story to please her? He has told me what it was as well as he is able, and from it I gather that Shepperton told him to say Nurse was unkind to him and that he loved Shepperton. The child, I suppose, would not, for I heard her say, ' I'll teach you to say that again,' and then whip him. Mr. Chalmers, I have put up with a great deal and had many disagreeables since my uncle's death, but I cannot and will not put up with *that*. I dislike Shepperton intensely, and she is no favourite with any of the servants, but I would never have noticed her if she had left the child alone."

" Of course you are doing right, there is no question about that, Miss Rudkin. The fault rests with her ladyship for not letting her maid go. She has had her a long time, I suppose ?"

" Certainly ever since she came here; she brought her, but I cannot say for how long before."

Lady Rudkin and her maid were to leave on Saturday morning, so it was announced, and Renie sent Christie to know what time she would like the carriage. This was the Friday night, and the girl came back with her ladyship's compliments, and would Miss Rudkin go and speak to her after dinner ?

Accordingly Renie went, and, to her surprise, my lady greeted her most amiably, and told Shepperton to leave them.

"I have decided, Miss Rudkin, to return to my aunt, and reside with her, at least for a while. I have sent my address to Mr. Chalmers; but I could not part with you in anger. That I have been badly treated, there is no denying; but I must forgive all injuries, as I hope to be forgiven."

Renie's lip curled. This was a new feature in my lady's character. But she made no reply, seeing that the oration was not all delivered.

"I have ever striven to keep peace and good feeling between us, Miss Rudkin, out of consideration to your position. When my dear late husband told me he had agreed to suffer you to live here, I made up my mind not to let you feel your painful position more than I could avoid, and there was plenty of room in the house for you. But I little guessed how my kindness was to be rewarded."

So lacerated were my lady's fine feelings that her essence bottle was required, and before the stopper was replaced Renie spoke. It was clearly a case of " diamond cut diamond."

" You are magnanimous, Lady Rudkin, but it is useless and unnecessary. I know you as well as you know yourself. Charity and humility consort badly with lying and deceit. But as you are disposed to show me the better side of your nature I have no objection, especially as I know how to value it. Yet there are several trifles that you are mistaken in, and oddly, too, since your late husband explained them differently to you. With regard to my coming here, it was *he* who proposed and *I* who agreed; I came at his desire. My position was painful, as you just now phrased it, but not because of shame or poverty—I have money, though little. But my position *was* painful, and all because I saw you in your true colours, which my uncle, poor old man, did not till it was too late. You did wisely not to pick a quarrel with me, and I forebore to show him the falseness of the wife he had chosen.   I think we may cry quits, Lady Rudkin."

The widow's face was drawn now, and all approach to meekness done away with; she was fairly beaten, and she saw it.

" You are severe, Miss Rudkin, and I need scarcely say, unjust.   But as I am going, let us be friends, let us part friends."

" That we have never been, and never can be now; but I will do you a kindness if ever it is in my power gladly, and always treat you with politeness for my uncle's sake.   Is there anything further than the carriage you desire, and at what time that?"

Lady Rudkin let her eyes fall.

" I am rather short of money, Miss Rudkin; could you lend me ten pounds?   And I should like the carriage at half-past nine in the morning."

Renie saw the drift of her sweetness.

" Yes, you can have ten pounds if you want

it, Lady Rudkin, and I will now wish you
good night. I will send the money to you
shortly."

Lady Rudkin extended her white hand,
which contrasted strangely with Renie's brown
one. They shook hands as a matter of form,
and Renie left her. She had never once asked
after her boy, or expressed any wish to see
him. It quite shocked poor Renie, and she told
them when she returned to the drawing room.
Miss Trufit shed tears, and prophesied something dreadful after such unnatural conduct.
Renie wished anything rather than that; the
servants would be sure to talk. She resolved
that she should see her child, and instead of
sending the sealed envelope by Christie, as
previously intended, she waited till half-past
eight the next morning, and sent the child
with it to his mother. He was to ask to see
mamma, and give it to her. The little fellow
went, but was not detained three minutes.
What sort of parting his mother gave him

Renie never knew, but she felt relieved when the close carriage drove off with Lady Rudkin and her maid. Thus it was she left the shelter of her kind husband's roof, believed by most of the servants to be going away for her health. It was all like a dream to Renie, as she looked at the boy romping about now so freely and entirely hers. His mother seemed if anything to be glad to get rid of him, at any rate it occasioned her no sorrow. Where she had gone was more than Renie knew, for Sir Bevis, in mentioning her aunt, named no place. It was not the sort of thing to happen in any respectable family, especially one like the Rudkins'.

CHAPTER XVII.

THE Count and Countess Helring had, since
Sir Bevis's sudden death, shown marked kindness to his widow, and they showed still more
after the departure of that widow.   They felt
for Renie, and the kind old Countess came
and had many and many a long chat with Miss
Trufit about her.   The Count, with the innate
delicacy and refinement common to foreigners,
made his visits more sparing till urged by
Renie to come oftener.   The friendly evenings passed together rendered the winter
months more agreeable, and with April

showers there came a decided change. One
day it rained love, and on only two people.
Lucy Northwood's face and good nature had
long ago bewitched the handsome Carl, and
since they had seen each other oftener he
fancied she liked him, so wisely resolved to
end the suspense by asking her. I am sure
his mother was not in the secret, yet one would
have thought it by the clever manner in which
she got Miss Priscilla out of the drawing-
room. Renie had already gone to see Rodney
in his snug crib. This was surely a most
favourable opportunity, and so the Count
seemed to think, for he edged a trifle nearer
to Miss Northwood.

Now that young lady was not expecting
such a thing, of course, and consequently her
ears got rosier as the handsome German got
nearer. What might have happened to those
little ears there is no means of deciding had
not the Count spoken just then.

" Miss Northwood, I have been regarding

you for a long time in silent admiration, do you know?"

"What an ass the man is," thinks Lucy, "just as if I could say yes!"

But it turned out that the Count's "Do you know" was not the end of a sentence, but the beginning, for he presently said—

"Do you know I love you, Lucy?"

This was certainly embarrassing, so Lucy did the most discreet thing—sighed, and waited to hear what more he had to say.

"Will you be my wife?" came the next question.

"Yes," replied Lucy, quietly.

Thereupon the Count said—

"Very well, my dear, and now I must ask your mamma's consent, and you must give me a kiss."

It afforded no little pleasure and amusement to all when their engagement was made known. Mrs. Troost said she had guessed it from the very first, and hoped Miss Lucy, poor thing, would like the snails them Germans ate, as she did not believe *she* ever should.

" Well, Lucy," said Renie, smiling, " I am pleased at your good fortune, dear, and I am sure you will be happy."

" Yes, I hope to be, Renie; I never should have married anything like a quarter so well but for you; you have been a sister to me. I only wish you were settled; I think all this anxiety is making you look ill."

" Nonsense. I am quite well," replied Renie, hastily. " And now, don't you want to go home after this conquest; they are sure to be expecting you, and the wedding is to be in the summer, so I am told."

" Yes, I think Carl wants it then, and we are to go abroad for awhile. Yes, I will go for a month or three weeks, but I will not leave you longer, Renie."

" Very well, my dear, though I should not take advantage of your absence to make love to Carl."

And Lucy went, having done all in her power to get Renie to go with her; it was just the season, Stars and Garters running wild. But nothing could induce Renie to desert her charge, who was getting a beautiful child. June was a glorious month, the cherries were hanging in ripe clusters from the drooping trees, and no time was so good as that when Renie played with the little boy amid the long grass, and chased butterflies. His merry, joyous shouts echoed through the trees and made their way to heaven, where surely they were welcome. Lucy had been away almost a month, and Renie began to think it would be nice to have her back again. The marriage was to take place at Zeigleheath; it was the Count's desire, and Lucy's mother and sisters could easily come down. Norman Howard would give her away, and Addy had decided that the wedding should be a very pretty one.

Meanwhile Rufus Sebastain had written to

Renie several times, and the last letters had
been full of some invisible joy that diffused
itself through the mind of the artist, and
altered the tone of his epistles. He said very
little about his work, and seemed to have
other ideas in view, of which he gave no clear
description. Yet it was evident that everything good was in the ascendant for the
artist. Renie was completely puzzled, and
gave him to understand so in her replies.
But it was all to no purpose; the cause of
the happiness did not come to light.

The summer was at its brightest and best
one morning shortly before Lucy was expected home. Renie was near an open
window, painting busily and listening to the
birds singing. A great stupid bee had found
its way into the room, and immediately got
mystified and could not find its way out, and
there it stayed, bumping its head against the
glass. It was the sort of morning when
every sound is heard with a laughing echo,

as if the fairies in the sun-beams wanted to keep it; the sort of morning when even nature seems bound to take a holiday.

Suddenly this lull was disturbed by another sound; a long dismal shriek, that came full into the room and made its presence felt. Renie flung down her brush and rushed out and down the stairs. There were Miss Trufit and Frost running in different directions.

" No, no, called Renie, it was outside, not in !"

They rushed from the hall and looked round; there was nothing to be seen but a woman coming from the trees by the river's side, with no hat, no bonnet, and her arms stretched wildly before her. It was nurse Mary, and there was no Rodney. Oh, where was the summer's morning for Renie, as she sank upon the lawn? The woman was coming crushing her way along madly as Renie staggered up and told them to run. Nurse seemed to see no one but her young mistress, and, falling on her knees before her, gasped, " Sir Rodney."   Down by the peaceful river there was nothing but cries and lamentation, there was no sign of the child, and old Frost said, " The rush is down to the mill; Miss Renie, he has drifted there." There they went, Renie running along the grassy bank by the old servant's side.   But they might have taken their time, for it was indeed " Too late."

The mill wheel was turning as steadily as ever, lashing the placid water into a white lather, and there, over a moss-covered stone projecting from the side of the mill, was the body of sweet little Rodney.   Hat was gone, and his cotton frock fluttered on the water. His golden head was pillowed on the soft green moss, and one fat hand grasped firmly a bunch of blue bells and rushes.   There was no look of terror on the sweet face ; he was half laughing, as no doubt he had been when the wicked waters sucked him in.

Renie gave one short, sharp cry as she saw him; she could not help it. She had learnt to love the gentle child so dearly, and she had had very little to love all her life. And now her trust was ended, stopped on a June morning, and those passive little fingers would never stroke her face again on this side Jordan. What he might have grown up there was no telling, and maybe the stream was good to take him on its bosom that early day. Frost carried him home so tenderly, the others crying, and the news flew like wild-fire.

" The little heir was drowned."

Norman and Addy, the Count and Countess, the clergyman, the curate, and even Doctor Bacup, but he was not received; all came in tears and horror to be greeted by Renie with a still, pale face, that as usual made Addy cry. She could say very little to them, except that the child lay prettier than ever, with his damp curls sticking to his little head in his crib upstairs, sleeping the sleep which knows no sorrow. Dr. Owen was attending nurse, and she was as yet unable to give any account of the sad accident.

"And now your trust is over, Renie?"

"Yes, it is, and I wish it had ended any other way; but God knows, Norman, I did my best for the dear child."

"Yes, we all know that, we have had proof of it. But things will all be upset again."

"Yes, only I shall be clear, my charge ceases now. That reminds me I will telegraph for Mr. Chalmers at once. I am half stunned, there has been nothing but anxiety of late; and Lady Rudkin must be sent for."

By degrees the house got quiet, and the people went. Addy asked if she should remain, but Renie preferred not. She was a good little soul, but Renie could not get on with her at all times; she quite unintentionally lashed her into a fury, and then cried.

Miss Trufit, who had been watching by
nurse with Mrs. Troost, came to Renie as the
evening closed in to ask her to see Mary, who
wished it very much. Renie was sitting by
the window, resting her head against the cool
stone, thinking of things past and things
present, and trying to define the future.

"Yes, I will go of course, Miss Priscilla;
but I do trust nurse is in no fault, because if
so I could never forgive her."

"My dear, just go and hear the poor
creature's touching story, and then judge.
She seems almost beside herself now that her
memory has returned."

What Miss Trufit said was perfectly the
truth; nurse was almost out of her mind,
and setting up in bed excitedly when Renie
entered.

Mrs. Troost was trying to get her to take
some gruel, but she would not.

"Oh! I do so wish Miss Renie would come,
it seems weeks since it happened, and you

say it is not a day. 1 know why my young mistress keeps away, Mrs. Troost, she thinks I am to blame, and she does not like to reproach me. I know Miss Renie well."

Renie had been standing in the shade, but she now came forward, and grasping one of the bed posts, said kindly—

" I wish you could rest, Mary, I think you would if you saw my pretty darling, he looks so happy."

The poor creature burst into a great sob, and wept freely.

"Miss Renie, do you blame old nurse? Tell me for God's sake. He knows I would have died for the lamb."

" I am sure of that, Mary; but it would not have been the same. He just wanted one little floweret, so fresh and sweet, to put in His crown. He wears a crown of flowers and jewels."

" Miss Renie, what's that you're saying?" asked the woman sharply.

" A blessed truth, Mary."

She looked at her doubtfully for a second,
and then her lips moved silently. Suddenly
she roused herself and said—

" Miss Renie, I want to tell you how it
happened. Will you give me a drink ?"

Mrs. Troost gave her it, and she went on—

" The Lord only knows how it came about,
for I don't. We had been gathering blue
bells and rushes to make a posy for you under
the ash tree, and I sat down with my back
against its trunk, the child by me. I went
on putting them together, him holding the
bunch, and presently he strayed a few steps
away from me, but I had no fear, for he never
went to the bank alone, little pet. A short
time and I called him, but he made no answer,
and I jumped up, just in time to see his little
frock whirling down the stream. I think I
lost my reason then, for I remember no more
till I found myself in this bed."

" You don't recollect screaming or meeting me, nurse ?"

" No, Miss Renie. I had only one idea, and that was Sir Rodney. But, now I am puzzling myself to think how it happened; he had not been gone five minutes, there was no scream, no splash. He was singing to himself, and he stopped suddenly, and that made me call. That is just how it was, Miss Renie, and when I stand before my maker He will not cast me away for neglecting that child."

It was a strange account, and nurse was not the only one puzzled. But it was little use speculating; the child, who perhaps could have told how it happened, was at peace. He was dead, and Zeigleheath once more without a master. Renie could not in all justice blame the poor faithful woman, who had nursed herself, and who was now suffering so acutely.

" No, nurse, I do not blame you; it is an accident, but a queer one. We must leave it till the time when every puzzle will be explained. Now go to sleep and let me find you much better in the morning. Mrs. Troost, someone must remain with her all night?"

"Very good, Miss Renie."

With the lamps came Mr. Chalmers.

"Bless us all, my dear Miss Rudkin, there seems no end to your troubles. How sad this is; poor little lad, poor little lad!"

"Yes, Mr. Chalmers, I feel quite sorrowed; he promised to be such a noble boy, and, worse than all, he was the last male in the Rudkin line. This place now goes to Leopold Gunstan!"

"To be sure, to be sure it does. Where is Mr. Gunstan? because he must be apprised of this?"

"I really don't know; his mother lives, or used to live, near Dolgelly. But I know no more, my uncle never told me. Mr. Gunstan is a great wanderer; it is more than seven months since I sent him from here."

" You sent him ?"

"Yes, I did, Mr. Chalmers. He is no favourite of mine, and he made himself too comfortable. So I disturbed him."

There was a tinge of red in the girl's face, and the attorney smiled oddly.

" Well, we must set about finding him, I suppose. And where are you going, Miss Rudkin ?"

It was the first time the idea had been presented to her in all that weary day. Where had she to go to ? Beach Cliff ? No, not there. And poor Miss Trufit, she, too, was homeless. Renie had now £200 a year, with what her uncle had left her, and it seemed a fortune to her, then she could work and make more. The business was where to live and how to buy furniture. Mr. Chalmers saw there was a difficulty.

" You know you need not go at once, not till Mr. Gunstan comes ; only the income is from to-day his."

" I don't want to remain longer than I can take to fix my plans, Mr. Chalmers. I know what I should like to do, but there is an obstacle in the way, and that is money. There is a pretty little cottage house on the road to the village to let, £30 a year; it belongs to some gentleman in London. I would take that and live there with Miss Trufit, only that I have no money to furnish, and I do not like to borrow even from Norman Howard."

" No, and very wise. But I fancy we can manage it, Miss Rudkin. There is a balance in hand, rightly the little heir's. You have not been spending the full income these last six months, as you well know, and now he is dead it is yours, as his guardian, and ought *not* to go to the next heir, Mr. Gunstan.

Why not furnish with that? It is your right, my dear young friend?"

"If you are sure it is, I will; I shall not want much?"

"There will be £120 or £130 when every expense is paid, I daresay. Just think about it, Miss Rudkin, and then let me know your decision; if it is to take this cottage I will see if it cannot be got cheaper for a term, three or five years. I am only sorry to have to part company with you so soon, Miss Rudkin. I hoped to see that child a man, and to have carried on the estate with you till then. But though that is at an end, I don't intend to let our acquaintance cease, and if ever you want advice or help I shall be glad to give it."

It was kindly meant, kindly spoken, and Renie truly thanked him.

He was a good-hearted man, and stayed over little Rodney's simple funeral. It was a joyful sad day that, for there was one on earth the less, one in Heaven the more, and tears fell from many eyes as the little coffin was sunk beside the old Baronet's, put there not eight months before. Lucy had returned immediately, and did her best to comfort poor Renie, who endured her trouble silently.

CHAPTER XVIII.

THE time went on, and no Leopold Gunstan
appeared, he was advertised for in all papers,
but to no purpose. There came a silly,
childish epistle from Lady Rudkin at the
time of Rodney's death, excusing herself
from attending the funeral on the grounds of
being ill from the shock. She was residing
with her aunt Mrs. Lofgan, who spoke of
going to the South of France shortly. No
one replied to this letter if Mr. Chalmers did
not, for it was sent to him. There were

great speculations as to where Mr. Gunstan had gone to, and Lucy coolly recommended Renie to tell Mr. Chalmers to ask my lady.

"Lucy! said Renie in astonishment, how can you dream of such a thing? Lady Rudkin knows no more of him than we do?"

"Glad you think so, for I don't. I shouldn't care to stake this ring on it, though I daresay Carl, dear blundering fellow, would give me another."

Whether Lucy's opinion was founded on fact there was no means of ascertaining, for neither one or the other came to the surface, and Renie determined to abandon Zeigleheath, now Fern Cottage was cleaned and repaired. Mr. Chalmers had seen after it for her, and had taken it for five years at £20 per annum. Now came the furnishing. Renie was very modest in her requirements, and everything was of the simplest and most inexpensive. The cottage was a pretty one, and contained

three sitting-rooms and four bedrooms. Addy
nearly killed herself trotting to and fro
putting things to rights, and it did really look
peaceful and cosy as she placed a vase of
flowers in the window, and waited the arrival
of its young mistress. The household was
spare, nurse and Christie Parnell being all the
servants. Mrs. Troost and Frost remained
at Zeigleheath to take charge of the house till
the owner should appear.

Miss Priscilla now showed her real worth ;
she saved and spared Renie in everything,
and left her undisturbed to her painting in the
little side room. Lucy stopped with them,
and the joyous Count kept perpetually appearing at doors and windows all day long.

He brought his zither, and sang Lucy love
ditties, while Renie listened and hoped sin-
cerely that two who were so good and kind
might pass a happy life together.

The last of Rufus Sebastain's epistles had

been rather desponding—in fact, melancholy. He expressed himself as much grieved to hear of the change, and called her his true friend. Renie wrote back a kind, cheerful letter, inviting the young man to Fern Cottage, and it had not been answered.

At the end of October, Lucy became Countess Helring. The day was fine, but cold, and they all assembled in the pretty church with nipped noses. The bride and bridegroom acquitted themselves admirably, and Carl was merrier than ever. Norman Howard gave Lucy away, the breakfast was at Beach Cliff, and at two o'clock the happy pair drove off amid a shower of old slippers. This little excitement over, a dead calm reigned at Fern Cottage, broken only by the merest trifles. Its inmates had no money to expend on amusement, and the days and months fled by, bringing with them the Count and Countess Helring, and more cares to Renie.

Leopold Gunstan could not be found, and his mother was dead. She died directly after Sir Bevis, and her poor furniture was sold to pay her debts. What had become of her handsome son, no one knew; he had not set foot in Dolgelly, to the people's knowledge, for years and years.

Sometimes Renie took a stroll up to Zeigle-heath, and saw Mrs. Troost, and the grand old place, so deserted and still.

There was now no laughter in the groves, no child's shout of glee, and the river ran clear and swift, rippling joyously over the soft pebbles, breaking here and there with a gurgle or splash—the same, and yet so different !

Lucy had been charmed with Carl's Hom-burg, and brought no end of beautiful things home with her. She and Addy spent a whole morning turning out the grandeur, and trying on Paris bonnets and hats, while Renie sat on the middle of the floor, surrounded by heaps of what she ignorantly called rags and rubbish, thereby bringing down upon her head the wrath of the good-hearted Lucy. Presently she got up and told them she was tired, and would go. Addy tried in vain to get her to put on a lovely bonnet. But it was useless; Renie could not admire the gorgeous affair, with a great bunch of bell fuchsias flopping about on her back. Addy and Lucy declared it was most graceful, so unstudied, not in the least like our hideous proud English bonnets. No doubt they were correct; it looked as if it had been put together in the dark, and all hung on one thread.

Renie said she was going home, and proceeded to do so the shore way. It was a lovely July day, and the sun glittered on the still water, from which there came scarcely a breeze. Renie walked along the soft sand, thinking of little Rodney, and what the year had been without him. When she did glance up, she perceived she was quite close to Zeigleheath. She had forgotten all about turning, and continued on the straight road. Well, she would go and see Mrs. Troost; that time was as good as any, since she was so near. But the day was so tempting, and the shade of the trees of the river so refreshing, that she sat down to rest a few moments before going to the house. The gentle summer breeze fanned her face and wafted her thoughts back to the time when the artist had sat there, that night when he had told the sad story of his early life so simply and touching. She fancied she could hear the pleasant voice now and then slightly tremulous as he confessed his poverty and unhappiness. She sat, her hands on her lap, and just thought how unequally this world's sweets were divided, and then of her love for this man. She had nothing to offer him but love, and he was ambitious, ah! if she only had position and money to offer, if—

"That was not the birds." She turned sharply to see the object of her thoughts, leaning against a tree. He was pale and dusty, weary and worn; her generous nature understood and saw it all; he was poor.

"Mr. Sebastain, come at last! I am glad to see you; but this is not my home now, I must take you to it. Miss Trufit has often watched for you."

She stopped; he had grasped her out-stretched hand and held it fast, but he did not appear quite conscious of what she was say-ing; one word only caught his attention.

"Home!" said he, laughing bitterly. "Home! there is no such place, at least, not for me."

Renie started; the tone was so strange, and his face looked hard and white, as if he had lost all feeling and passed many sleepless nights.

"What is the matter with you, Mr. Sebas-tain?"

He stared at her, and then taking off his hat, said—

"I thought everyone knew my shame and degradation. But I forgot, perhaps it may be news to you. Let us sit here, Miss Rudkin, and I will confess my sins and faults, like a good boy. You are a patient creature, God knows! and don't shrink from me; so I feel free to tell you. Ah! if this wind would only blow it away, and leave me as if it had never been; if I could only blot it out."

Renie asked no questions; she waited till he was calmer and ready to tell.

"When the wind blows in from the sea, as the song says, I wonder what it brings? This gentle wind brings back to me the first day I came here, Miss Rudkin; and us sitting

here that night while I told of my early days
of misery and vagabondizing. I remember
what you told me; how you lent me a help-
ing hand as only a woman can do; but it is
a different sort of story I have got to tell you
to-day."

"Go on, I am listening; but I did not
imagine anything to be wrong with you, from
the tone of your letters. Those letters
mystified me, Mr. Sebastain; what made you
so happy ?"

"Ah! you may well ask, I believe I was
dreaming; in fact, I must have been, Miss
Rudkin, or else our forefathers and the Bible
are mistaken, and women are hypocrites and
liars. Miss Rudkin, I have just learnt a
useful but bitter truth; I hope you'll never
learn it. Listen. I have been in love, for
that matter am now, and ever shall be, and
with a lady of noble birth. I was a fool, and
she was a beautiful—devil, I cannot call her

anything else. Lady Constance Butler let
me love her; made me believe she loved me;
nay, told me so—shame be unto her false
heart—and then cast me off; cast me off like
a pet she was weary of, because an earl
with a coronet came to her feet. She did
not care what I suffered; she did not care for
my blasted life; and when I taxed her with
her baseness, her cruelty, she turned and
scoffed at me for my presumption in daring to
love her; me, a poor outcast, with even no
parents to own me—a poor wandering artist.
She might have spared me further, I was
already humbled enough; but no, I must be
made to see my proper place, to prevent mistakes in future. So she had told her family
and her lover, and they were *amused*. It got
abroad how I had dared to love the Lady
Constance Butler, and the fat rich men
laughed over their wine at that ' poor devil of
a Spaniard.' So I am hunted away, pitied

and scoffed at, and yet I love her more than my life. I have lost my hope; I am deceived by the lovely cold creature, as false as she is fair, and still I love her."

His head sank upon his hands, and the tears dropped from between his fingers on the dry path. He was crying, grieving for his false base love. He had never glanced at Renie once while he hurried over his story, and it was well he did not. I don't know that that July sun looked upon such another face as that girl's in all the wide world. I hope it did not.

There are moments as black as night in the lives of most people, when even the tender love and mercy of our Father fades away, and we lose our hold on Christ when we begin to question the reality of that Divine power.

That dense cloud of misery and darkness was over Renie now, it had drawn the broad brow into a hard knot and nipped in the mouth, overspreading the quiet face with a ghastly hue.

Was there a God in Heaven? Were there any Angels? If so, where their pity? their mercy? What did they think of what they saw? Her loving him with all her soul, ready to work and strive, contented on half the allowance allotted to another and yet denied it.

To see him crushed and wounded, crying like a child for his love, and not be able to offer him hers, which was deep and strong enough to endure anything; which, if put by the side of many a woman's would, by reason of its unsullied purity and unselfishness, have shown hers dross.

And he did not want it. She must listen to his sorrows and see him grieve, and never say a word; she was his sister, his friend. Why had God let it happen? Why?—

Hush! he is moving, and the white haggard face shows so clearly against the green leaves that droop over the rustic seat, that something like tears start to the girl's eyes and lends them a beautiful softness which gradually spreads over her face.

Aye! when the great day of reckoning comes and accounts are settled, there will be something to the credit of that girl who, in the bitterness of her own sorrow, helped the one who had caused it, with no other feeling in her breast than tender pity. Forbearing to utter one hard word against him or his love, regardless of her own hurt, mindful only of his.

Rufus Sebastain sighed deeply—

"You are very silent, Miss Rudkin."

"I think silent sympathy is best; I don't know what to say to you to soften the cruel blow. It would be mockery to bid you forget, so I can only hope that Time with his healing wings may cure you."

He got up and stood looking at her fixedly; there was something strange in the white face of his ministering angel that he could not understand.

" Come, Mr. Sebastain, let us go home ; but it is only a poor little place."

No home was poor where she was; it was richer than many a King's palace, and she would take the poor cast-down artist there and make him happy while she could. He made no resistance; he seemed tired, weary of wandering about, and they set off together. She showed him the place where Rodney was drowned; but he was no doubt thinking of the wicked Lady Constance, for he offered very little sympathy.

He was different to her, his own trouble was uppermost, and he could not think of hers. But she made no reproach, only gently led him along to her cottage home, thankful to get him there.

Miss Trufit dropped her work and went to

meet him gladly. He had found a place in
the old lady's heart; she spake of him as that
" poor boy !"

" Why, this is a pleasant surprise; we
thought you had deserted us. Where did
Renie find you ? She finds every one."

" Yes," replied he, smiling wearily, " Miss
Rudkin finds all the stray sheep, and this
time it is a black one."

" Nay, nay, now you are gloomy; and,
bless us all ! how thin you've got ! If you
don't fatten sharply you'll disgrace us."

Miss Priscilla put his miserable appearance
down to too hard work, and told everyone so,
and neither he nor Renie undeceived them.
But one morning, after he had been there a
week, he came into the little painting room
and asked Renie what she had been doing.

" Ah, I have done plenty, and sold them all
but what you see. I am doing very well in
a quiet way, and it is a nice help. And now
about yourself."

"I knew you would ask me that, and I have been dreading it, because I cannot give a good account of my time. I have been idle and done nothing but scraps to sell and enable me to live and keep up appearances. You have improved your time, I see, and, of course, get a better price."

"Slightly. But why not begin something now while you are here, Mr. Sebastain?"

He was silent a second and then said, dejectedly—

"No, Miss Rudkin, it is too late; I cannot look things in the face; I have not got your resolution; I am going abroad to try my fortune there."

Renie dropped her brush and faced him, a flush on her pale cheek.

"What! you are going abroad to drivel your time away, all because you are disappointed. I would not be trod on by a woman, if I were you. You will never do anything beyond existing if you go away, I know full well, and what will she care?"

He made no answer, but twitched the columbine that clustered round the open window; she could rouse neither anger nor pride; Lady Constance had done her work well, truly!

He remained leaning out of the casement, watching the wind blow the long grass in the meadow, just the sort of grass for happy children to bathe their dollies in. At last he broke silence, but never turned his face.

" You are correct, Miss Rudkin, I shall do nothing creditable, I shall disappoint you. And yet I did set to work so hopefully, and did well till the cursed day I saw her beautiful face. She has been my drag, my torment, and I cannot face the people again and expect them to buy my pictures after my presumption. I feel so crushed. Do you know," and he turned quickly, " she taunted me with my solitary condition, having no family to mention, though ever so humble. Miss Rudkin, I envy the costermonger boys in the street, because they can point to the man at the pony's head and call him ' father.' I would gladly own my father, could I find him, if he were only a Spanish muleteer. No, I cannot go back to London ; I must make a fresh start, and perhaps I shall find a place to lay my head in."

Tears were again in his eyes, and, had it not been for Renie's great love for him, she might have smiled, for there is something contemptable in a chicken-hearted man. But this one was different to the rest ; he had been alone all his life, and uncared for, and now he had given the pent-up love of a lifetime to a proud, cold-hearted beauty, who flung it back in his face and jeered at him.

The look of pain came into Renie's eyes again as she watched him ; it had been a long,

long week to her. She had passed it driving
her love down to the bottom of her heart,
because she saw and felt it would never be
asked for. That might be got over, for Renie
had not been used to having her desires gra-
tified, but how about losing sight of him?
Letting him wander far away, and perhaps
never see him again? She felt she could behold his happiness and make no sound, but she
could not endure the waste, the desolation
that would come when she lost him. And yet
she had no power to make him stay; if he
would not work she could not keep him: it
was a hard trial.

"Have you any friends, Mr. Sebastain, in
Spain?"

"Not one; I have no friends."

"And I suppose no money?"

He was silent, and a faint pink mounted to
his pale face.

"You need not mind telling me," said she,

touching his sleeve, " have you no money
saved ?"

The pink deepened to red.

" No," said he, huskily, " I haven't a
penny, " I have even spent the nest egg, *your*
money."

There was a second stillness, and then her
voice said, in a cheerful, kindly tone—

" Never mind, there are more nest eggs
than one. You cannot go without money;
tell me how much you have got."

He was not begging, reader, don't think
that; he was proud and would not have told
his poverty to another had he starved, but he
yielded to this girl without a murmur.

He put his hand into his pocket and pulled
something out, which Renie coolly took from
him and proceeded to count.

He was off, brooding on his sorrow again,
for he never looked, and seemed not to know
what she was doing. She held a little heap

of rubbish. A few pieces of soiled paper, a key, one sovereign, two half crowns, and three pennies; sum total, £1 5s. 3d. A large amount to go abroad with, barely enough to pay his fare back to London. Renie put it on the table with a clink.

"Mr. Sebastain, I wish you would pull your head in and listen to me for a moment. This is all you have! How can you talk of going abroad with this? Yet you say you must go, and so do I, since you won't work here; but you must have money, therefore I must be your banker as far as I am able."

"But, Miss Rudkin,"—

"Hush! I cannot lend you much, because I am not rich, but I can lend you seventy pounds; I have made it this year out of my pictures."

"I cannot take your money, Miss Rudkin. It shames me that you, a girl, should work and have money, while I have none."

"Ah, but you have been ' keeping up appearances,' doing as other people do, regardless of the difference in your positions. If I got as many dresses as Addy or Lucy, I should not have seventy pounds this minute. Ease your mind, Mr. Sebastain, I can spare it and make it again if I have health, and you must take it. Now, when are you going?"

" The sooner the better, I suppose, Miss Rudkin, since you provide me the means, which I hope to return in a few months. This week: a day will suffice to get my things together at my lodgings; I will leave here on Thursday and start on Saturday."

It was fixed there and then and duly made known. Miss Trufit tried to persuade him to remain, and called upon Renie to support her, but that young lady was mute. She felt it was better that he should go—better for him decidedly, perhaps better for her, but that was not of much consequence either way. The parting was a quiet one; how could it be otherwise when Renie was too proud to either faint or cry? She only looked awfully white, and attributed that to the heat. She spoke kindly to him, and he grasped her hand, and promised to write as before.

"And my letters shall not be like the last, Miss Rudkin."

Thus they parted, those two, each unconscious of what was to follow when the sea rolled between them.

Renie locked the door to exclude visitors, and tried to think, but the tears would fall, and she could only cry for her love with a silent voice. He was all to her, she was nothing to him. She thought of the last parting, and what he had said about the tide. Oh, if it would only erase his image from her mind; his name from her heart. But alas! they were not printed on sand.

With the close of the hot day she went upstairs and got ready for tea, at which Miss Trufit chatted incessantly, but, fortunately, did not expect Renie to answer—a word was sufficient to keep her going. And then came the silent night, when no one watches, and there was no need to hide her face, since it was a relief to let her agony be written there. A relief to stretch her arms across the window-sill, and cry to the soft night wind, "My darling! my darling!" But there was no foolish outburst, and she spoke coolly to people who asked questions. They did not seem to consider it at all strange that he and Renie should be friendly, and that she should take an interest in him. It was only what her uncle had done.

Rufus Sebastain kept his word to write, and said he had taken a post in Italy for a short time, but that he should move on before long. Renie was only too pleased to learn that he had employment, it was a pity for such talent to be wasted.

END OF VOL. II.

T. C. NEWBY, 30, Welbeck Street, Cavendish Square, London.

www.ingramcontent.com/pod-product-compliance
Lightning Source LLC
Chambersburg PA
CBHW030640030726
47497CB00006B/1886